Bobbi Smith

writing as JULIE MARSHALL

Haven

LEISURE BOOKS   NEW YORK CITY

A LEISURE BOOK ®

January 2005

Published by

Dorchester Publishing Co., Inc.
200 Madison Avenue
New York, NY 10016

ISBN 0-8439-5312-8

Printed in the United States of America.

Visit us on the web at www.dorchesterpub.com.

This book is dedicated to all my friends who have been there for me through the years. Thanks for all your support.
Thanks, too, to Francoise and Renae at the Chanel Counter at Famous Barr. They did a "makeover" on me and it was wonderful!

HAVEN

CHAPTER ONE
DAY ONE

The Lord Be with You. . .

Darrell Miller's shoulders were hunched against the bite of the early December wind, and his collar was turned up to shield his face. He seemed to be just another of the poor men who shambled their way to work every morning down this main street of the city's once well-to-do north side. None of the others on the street paid any attention to his passing, and that was fine with him.

He paused at the corner to glance back the way he'd come. Only then did his nervousness reveal itself. There was a grimness to his expression and a wariness in his dark eyes that set him apart. He was no mere working man heading for his job. He was a hunted man—

Behind him, the street appeared normal. Traffic was the same as always. Yet he knew there was

1

no safety on this corner. He had to keep moving. He had to hide, to disappear.

Shoving his hands deeper into his pockets, Darrell started off again. He wasn't sure where he was going. He just couldn't let them find him . . . not after last night.

Memories of the horror he'd accidentally witnessed assaulted him, and he mentally prepared himself for what was to come. Though he longed to believe there was hope, he knew there could be no hiding from them forever. They were relentless. They would never give up looking for him.

Silently he cursed God for what had happened. At twenty-three, he was an ex-con who was trying to build a new life for himself, but he realized now that he might as well be dead. They would never let him live. Not with what he knew.

He'd taken a job on the late shift hoping to steer clear of the ugliness of the drug gangs. Yet the events of last night had proven to him how stupid he'd been to think he could escape his old life. He'd tried to avoid any contact with his old "friends," staying as far away as he could. But in spite of all his efforts, he was trapped now, and he doubted he would be able to break free.

Why now? he agonized as he continued on down the street, fighting the urge to run, to flee to safety. There was no safety for him. There never would be again.

Darrell heard a car coming. Rather than glance

up to see who it was, he kept his face averted, wanting anonymity. The car seemed to be slowing. Terror ate at him. *Was it them? Had they found him already?*

He did not want to die. Not now! Not like this! He could hear the car closing on him. His heart was pounding as his adrenaline surged. He was desperate—

The church bell pealed, ringing out only once to signal the half hour.

The sound startled Darrell to the awareness that he was standing at the bottom of the few steps that led to the doors of the old Catholic church. It was a massive building, constructed some hundred years before when this part of the city had been growing and thriving. Except for the steeple, the church was mostly devoid of external decoration. All that marked it as a House of God were the leaded, stained-glass windows that glowed softly from the inner light and the name of the parish, Our Lady of Perpetual Help, carved into the cornerstone.

Darrell was no Catholic, but right now with the car almost upon him, he was considering conversion.

Desperate for a place to hide, he climbed the few steps and let himself in. The heavy door closed solidly behind him, and he was enveloped by a sense of warmth and safety.

"The Lord be with you," a priest intoned from the altar.

"And also with you." The answer of the sparse

gathering of parishioners seated randomly in the pews for the daily 6:30 Mass echoed in the cavernous interior.

The church had been there forever, for all Darrell knew, but he'd never been inside it before. The beauty of the place surprised him, but he didn't have time to think about it. He needed to disappear, to vanish. He moved forward a few rows and slid into a pew close to a side door in case he needed to make a quick exit. There were several other worshipers nearby, but he didn't pay any attention to them.

He faced forward.

He did not look back.

For all that most of this part of town was starting to fall down, Our Lady of Perpetual Help Church stood as testimony to the beauty that could still exist in the world. The ceilings were high and arched. The walls were painted pristine white, and the ornate trim was gilded. Biblical scenes were highlighted in a rainbow of colors in the stained-glass windows, and the faint scent of incense hung in the air. There was something different about this place—something otherworldly.

Darrell had no idea what Catholics did, except kneel and stand and kneel and sit. He figured as long as he was halfway hidden there in a side pew, he could watch the others, follow their example, and look as if he belonged.

The front door opened again, and Darrell tensed. He cast a glance in that direction, fearing it was his pursuers, dreading what might happen next. He was prepared to run, to flee for his life.

Despair threatened to overwhelm him. Was he not even safe here in this House of God? Was there no haven? No safety for him? Even as the questions tormented him, he knew the answer. He edged closer to the aisle, watching, waiting—

A woman appeared, moving slowly up the aisle. Her movements were awkward, for she was burdened by the life she carried within her.

Darrell almost let out an audible sigh of relief. It was just a pregnant woman.

The woman felt his gaze upon her and glanced his way. She smiled at him, the smile transforming her weary expression into one of warmth and beauty. She mouthed a silent hello to him as she slipped into the pew just ahead of him.

Darrell pretended to turn his attention back to the altar, but he studied the woman for a moment out of the corner of his eye. She was young and pretty. It was obvious that she would soon have the baby, for her coat would not button over the mound of her stomach. He wondered why, heavy as she was with child, she had chosen to come to church on this cold, miserable morning. He would have stayed home in bed.

The priest's voice interrupted his thoughts, and Darrell forced himself to pay attention. He remained where he was, biding his time, dreading the moment when the Mass would end and he'd be forced to go back outside. In his heart, he hoped the service would last forever. At least in this place, he knew he was safe.

Jenny Emerson was glad when the reading began and she could sit down. As hard as the pew was, it still felt good to be off her feet. She took a deep breath, searching for calm, seeking inner peace, but found none. Instead the same terrifying thoughts that had hounded her for days echoed in her mind. How had she let her life come to this? She was twenty-two years old. She should have known better! What was she going to do?

With an effort, Jenny fought down the black, strangling fear that had been threatening to overwhelm her. Focusing instead on the reading, she concentrated on the words of hope and prayed that they were meant for her.

Her baby gave a vigorous kick, and Jenny rested a hand on her stomach in a loving caress. With a kick like that, she was almost certain the child was a boy. They had done a test at the clinic and the nurses knew the baby's sex, but she had refused to be told. She wanted to learn at the time of birth. Birth should be exciting and thrilling and happy and—

For one moment, the dreamer in Jenny allowed her to pretend that all was right in her world. Then the truth of her situation returned, just as it always did.

She was almost ready.

In a few weeks, she would be giving birth.

Jenny's mouth twisted bitterly as she struggled to hold back the scalding tears that threatened. There could be no avoiding the truth. There weren't always "happily ever after" endings.

Jenny sighed. She had come to Mass today because the end was near and she had to make a decision. Soon, very soon, she would give birth to the beautiful child she carried.

Her baby—

She smiled faintly, her face lighting with inner beauty for an instant before she frowned at the thought of the baby's father, the man she loved—or at least had thought she loved.

Mark—

Jenny wondered where Mark was, then told herself it didn't matter. He was out of her life. This baby was hers, not his. As far as she was concerned, he had forsaken any claim to the child the moment the check to pay for the abortion had arrived.

Their last conversation was still clear in her mind and painful to remember, even after all this time. . . .

"Jenny?"

"What do you want?" she'd replied, hoping he *wouldn't notice how raw her voice was from crying.*

"Did you get the check?"

"It came yesterday." She'd kept her answer short, *not trusting herself to say more, afraid of what she might blurt out, of what she might reveal.*

"Are you taking care of it?"

7

At his refusal to say the word baby or abortion, anger had grown within her. She'd used that powerful, sustaining emotion to get through the rest of the conversation and through the rest of these last few months.

"Don't worry, Mark," she'd managed with tight control. "I'll take care of 'it.' You don't have a thing to worry about."

"Jenny . . ."

He'd sounded concerned, and for a moment Jenny let herself hope. But that had been the last time.

"You don't need me to go with you or anything? My mother said—"

"I don't need you or your mother, Mark. Please don't call me again. There's really no point in our speaking anymore."

She'd hung up on him, quickly, quietly.

There had been no reason to say anything else.

His check had said it all.

He would go on with his life. She would go on with hers.

And she had.

And she had done fine.

Until yesterday, when the doctor had confirmed that her delivery date was only weeks away.

Until that moment, she'd believed she could do it. She'd believed she could make her life work—that she could have this baby and raise it alone. But suddenly with the event almost upon her, she was frightened, truly frightened.

What was to become of her? Of her baby?

And that was why she had come to Mass. She

had made some foolish choices all those months ago when she'd surrendered her innocence to Mark.

She had thought he loved her.

She'd thought they would marry.

It had been devastating to learn that she'd been wrong.

She had come here to God. God was her last hope. There was no one else she could turn to.

As Father Beck began to read the gospel, the impeccably dressed Dorothy Pennington stood straight and tall as she always did in the third pew from the front, center section. A pillar of the community, a member of the Legion of Mary and the Parish Council, Dorothy had devoted her life to her family and her church, and it was the latter that was holding her together this morning. No one looking at her would have guessed at the fragile state of her emotions and the despairing direction of her thoughts.

"Praise to you, Lord Jesus Christ," she answered as Father Beck concluded the gospel.

Dorothy sat down, smoothing her skirt over her knees in an unconsciously elegant gesture. She knew she should listen to every word of Father Beck's homily. She schooled her expression to one of respectful attention as she gazed up at the priest, but in truth, she couldn't concentrate, not on his sermon, not on anything. Deny it as she might, the pain was there within her, tearing at her heart with savage claws, ravaging her soul, destroying her world. She had no reason to breathe, no reason to exist—

Last night, Alan had left her.

"I want a divorce," he had said.

She had just walked into the house from her monthly meeting of the Parish Council.

The time on the clock had been 10:01.

Funny how she remembered that. She didn't know why she remembered. She just did.

Dorothy wondered, as she sat there motionless in the pew, if her distress showed. She wanted to shout and scream that this couldn't be happening to her. She had tried to be the perfect wife, the perfect mother, the perfect friend. She had tried to please Alan in every way she could. Dear God, they'd been married thirty-two years. Why was Alan doing this to her *now*—now, when the children were gone and their life together could have been better than ever since they had time to concentrate on each other again?

She had faced him calmly last night, wanting answers from him, getting none.

"That's not funny."

"I wasn't joking," he'd replied.

She'd stared at him then, shocked by his declaration. "Why, Alan? What's wrong? I didn't know you were unhappy."

"I didn't either, until I met Tina."

And at the look on his face when he'd said the girl's name, Dorothy had wanted to hit him, to curse him for his stupidity and for the pain he was causing her. In-

10

stead she'd tightened the legendary control she had over herself.

"May I ask where you met this other woman?" Dorothy knew her tone had been haughty, but she'd had good reason. Her world was being destroyed by this faceless woman who wanted her husband.

"Does it matter?" he'd challenged defensively.

"It matters." Her words had been terse.

"She transferred in from the office in L.A." He'd let his voice trail off as if he didn't want to say too much.

Dorothy's mind had been racing. True, they hadn't made love often in the last year or so, but Alan had never been a particularly lustful man. She had thought their love life was fine. He had been tender and caring and considerate. She had never felt a lack. How could she have been so blind?

"I see." She'd finally choked out the words. Then, desperate to get away from him before her dignity failed her, she'd ordered coldly, "Get out."

"Get out?" Alan had stared at her, a look of shock on his face.

"Now. Tonight. Your lawyer will be hearing from mine."

She'd turned away from the sight of him, praying he would leave, praying he would stay, praying he would fight for what they'd shared and built together over all the years of their marriage. They were in their fifties now. They were supposed to be looking forward to their golden years together. She'd held her breath, waiting for his response.

To her horror, he'd left without another word.

Dorothy had stayed up all night. She'd tried to understand it, and for a while, she'd blamed herself. She'd paced the floor in endless frustration when she could find no ease for her heartbreak. It had still been dark, black as pitch outside, when she'd left the house. After the long hours of torment, she had known that she had nowhere else to go.

She'd come to Mass.

Joe Myers stood with his head bowed as he tried to concentrate on the Eucharistic prayer Father Beck was offering up in preparation for Communion. Some days he listened, and it touched his heart. Other days, like today, the prayer was nothing but words strung together. Words, words, words. What good were words without action to back them up?

It was then that Joe realized how very angry he was this morning. He had said the rosary upon rising, as he always did. The prayers were dear to his heart, and he would continue to say them until he was physically unable to do so, but when he had glanced at the headlines in the paper as he'd left the house, he'd grown furious. Again overnight, people had been killed on the streets for no good reason, shot down in cold blood for what little money they had on them. Murder—rape—abuse—hatred. Was there no end to the misery? Didn't his prayers help—even a little?

He wondered if anyone besides him saw the

beauty of God's world? If anyone besides him looked in other folks' eyes and saw the potential there for goodness and love?

His anger was heated by his frustration. He was almost sixty-five years old. He would soon be going home—and that was just fine with him, as long as God figured he'd done a good job once he got there. But sometimes, he felt as if he'd failed in some way and he didn't know why.

Joe counted his blessings as Father Beck prepared to give Communion. Joe had Gail, his lovely wife of forty-odd years, and two beautiful, happy children with children of their own. Why had he been so blessed while others had not? Certainly, Joe knew God well enough to know that He didn't discriminate. God wanted everyone to be happy. And Joe knew he'd certainly been no saint. Why, then, had he been given so many joys in life while those around him were so lost and frightened?

Faith, Joe concluded.

It all had to do with faith. If you had faith, you could do anything, suffer anything, deal with anything.

Without faith—

Joe shuddered at the thought.

Life without faith in God would be a life not worth living. The whole purpose of life, as Joe saw it, was to do the best one could with what one had, helping others along the way. Smiles and helping hands were free, and they were two of the most powerful tools given to mankind.

"The peace of the Lord be with you always," Father Beck intoned.

"And also with you," Joe replied.

"Let us offer each other a sign of peace."

Joe smiled and, turning, lifted a hand in greeting to those spread out in the church around him.

He recognized most of those in attendance. The gang at 6:30 Mass were a hardy lot. It took a lot of initiative to get out of bed while it was still dark outside and come to church. You had to want to be there. He knew he did. He loved the peace of it. The solemnity of it. The centering of it. It was, to him, a wonderful thing to begin the day with God and dedicate the day to God. He figured those around him felt that way, too.

His gaze met Dorothy Pennington's, and they smiled at one another across the width of the church. Joe liked Dorothy. He had worked with her on numerous parish committees and activities. He thought she was one classy lady.

Joe caught sight of young Jenny Emerson off to the side toward the back of the church. Though he had been acquainted with her parents through the parish before they'd passed away several years before, he didn't know Jenny well. He had spoken with her and her boyfriend at one of the festivals the parish sponsored some months ago, but hadn't seen much of her since. Now, there was no mistaking her obviously pregnant state, and he hadn't heard that she'd married. He hoped all was well with her.

He spotted several others he knew by sight but not by name; there were a few other people he didn't know at all.

Joe was glad they were there.

Heaven was open to everyone, just like Our Lady was.

CHAPTER TWO

Darrell watched as the Catholics filed forward to take Communion. He saw his chance to disappear, and he took advantage of it. He stepped from the pew and moved to the side door. A gut feeling stopped him, and he offered up a quick, silent prayer before quietly slipping outside. It occurred to Darrell that it had been a very long time since he'd said any kind of prayer at all.

The sky was just beginning to brighten, so Darrell stayed close to the building he made his way around to the back. He might have been safe for the time he'd been inside, but he was on the street again now, and he had to be careful. He moved furtively down the still-dark passageway between the church and the rectory.

"Are you looking for someone?"

At the sound of the deep voice, Darrell froze. Gut-wrenching fear stabbed at him. Only after the dim light near the rectory door was turned on and he saw the kindly looking priest standing in the doorway did he relax a little.

"No. I was just cutting through to the alley. That's all." He spoke too quickly, his nervousness obvious.

"If there's anything you need, you have only to ask," the gentle-voiced man of God offered.

"I don't need anything but to get outta here." He ducked his head and started off again.

"I'm Father Walters," the priest called after him. "I'll be here tomorrow, if you want to come by and talk." The priest did not know if the young man heard him or not, for he had already disappeared into the last remnants of the darkness.

Darrell didn't answer or look back as he headed for the alley. The last thing he wanted to do was to start talking to some priest. Was the man crazy, talking to strangers like that? Didn't he know how dangerous it could be?

Darrell shook his head as he reached the end of the church and paused before stepping out into the alley. He glanced carefully both ways, saw no vehicles or people. He drew a deep breath of relief.

"Thanks, God," he muttered aloud, surprising even himself.

If he could avoid meeting anyone and get home safely, he'd be all right. Claire was there. Claire was waiting for him. He would go home to her. She was probably wondering where he was.

Darrell headed home, taking back streets all the way.

* * *

"Mass is ended. Go in peace to love and serve the Lord."

"Thanks be to God."

Jenny made her way slowly, awkwardly, from the pew and started out the main door. She'd been surprised when she'd come back from Communion and found the strange man gone. Usually if people were going to sneak out early, they did it after Communion, not before. She shrugged and thought no more of it. She had too many other things to worry about—like the fact that her car was still in the shop and she'd have to take the bus to work today.

"Good morning, Jenny."

The sound of a man's voice almost made her jump, and she glanced back to find Joe Myers following her.

"Good morning, Mr. Myers," she replied softly, keeping her tone quiet, for they were still in church.

"How are you feeling?" Joe asked as he held the door open for her to go outside.

"Fine." Embarrassment stung her as she moved past him. Jenny didn't want to talk about her condition, and so she didn't stop walking. "I've got to get on to work."

"Well, you take care," he said sincerely.

"You, too."

The very real warmth in Joe's words stayed with Jenny as she beat a hasty retreat down the steps. Her parents had often mentioned what good people Joe Myers and his wife Gail were, and she sensed they were right. There was something special about the older man, something very—almost holy, she thought. He seemed to glow with goodness, if that were possible. Jenny hurried up the block toward the bus stop.

Joe stopped at the top of the steps and watched the young woman go. He offered up a silent prayer that God would watch over her that day.

Glancing back then, Joe expected to find Dorothy right behind him. He was surprised to find that she'd already disappeared. He frowned, wondering where she could have gone so quickly. He'd expected to chat with her for a while.

With a shrug, Joe buttoned his coat against the chill waiting for him once he left the sheltering haven of Our Lady. He moved down the steps away from the church and out onto the sidewalk.

Joe glanced up as he went.

The cross at the top of the steeple made an impressive silhouette against the cloudy sky.

Joe headed for work.

"Where have you been?" Claire demanded when Darrell finally trudged up the steps to their second-floor apartment.

"I worked late," he lied, not wanting her to know the truth, wanting to protect her from the ugliness that surrounded and threatened him.

"Ambition. I like that in a man," she said with a smile as she went to him. She was only half dressed and in a rush, trying to get ready to go to work herself, but she always had time to kiss him. Claire had loved Darrell since they'd first met, and she had waited for him while he'd done his time. Now that he was back, she was determined they would never be apart again.

"Oh, baby," he groaned, taking full advantage of her invitation, sweeping her into his arms and holding her to his heart. "I love you."

"I love you, too," she whispered, drawing his head down to her for a kiss. "I miss you at night." It was a purr that promised him ecstasy.

Darrell needed no more invitation. He needed the affirmation that there was some sanity, some joy in his world. He needed to lose himself in the heat of her body, to believe for just a little while that he could have a better life. God only knew what the next few hours or days might bring. He needed Claire, and he needed her now.

There was a very real desperation in his lovemaking, but Claire, unaware of his torment, thought it was passion. She responded fully to his touch as she always did, giving him all the joy she could, seeking to please him in every way. She wanted to make him happy, to make him realize that they were wonderful together. When, at last, their passion was spent, they lay together in each other's arms.

Darrell held Claire close. His arms circled her possessively. He had never known such beauty as he found in her embrace. He lived in terror that he might lose her. She had become his world, his reason for existing. When everyone else had given up on him, she had believed in him. He had promised her he would do the right thing from now on, and he had meant every word of his promise.

"I have to go," she said, her voice soft with regret. Still, she made no move to leave.

"I know," he sighed, reluctant to free her, yet knowing that he must.

"You gonna miss me today?" she asked, trailing a hand over his chest.

"If you keep that up, you'll never find out, 'cause I won't let you go."

Claire gave a throaty laugh as she rolled away from him. She moved quickly to gather up her clothes, which had been hastily discarded about the room, and then disappeared into the bathroom to start getting ready for work all over again. "I'll get back as soon as I can, but I'm scheduled to work 'til five-thirty. Are you due back in at eight again?"

"Yeah."

She didn't notice the curtness of his answer. She was too busy getting ready. "Well, at least we'll have an hour or two together before you have to go."

"I'll be waiting for you."

"Get some sleep," she advised as she appeared before him fully dressed and ready to leave.

Darrell stared up at her, thinking how beautiful she was. Long-legged, well-built, she had the face of an angel and the heart of one as well. Darrell loved her more than life itself.

Claire bent to him and kissed him, a quick, soft peck before hurrying out of the three-room efficiency. "I'll see you later."

"Be careful," he called after her, but the door was already closing.

He got up and locked the door, then turned on the small black-and-white TV.

"In other news, a body was discovered this morning . . ." the news anchor was saying.

Darrell stared at the television set, wondering what he was going to do. There was no one he could talk to, no one he could go to. He was trapped, powerless before the forces that threatened him.

"Why?" he whispered in a tormented prayer that went unanswered.

"You're sure?"

"I'm positive. I saw the son of a bitch. He was coming up the street just as I took care of our little business."

"You got a good look at him?"

The man shrugged. "Good enough, I guess."

"What does 'I guess' mean?"

"No mistake, boss. If I see him again, I'll know him."

"You make it a point to see him again. I don't need this kind of trouble. I have business to conduct."

"Consider it taken care of." There was a deadly promise in his statement.

"I hope you do a better job on this than you did on your first attempt."

"I will."

The boss looked less than convinced, but said nothing as the other man left the room.

CHAPTER THREE

It was almost 7:00 A.M. Mark Seton stood at the window of his bedroom, staring out across the city. It was a cold, gloomy day, with a heavy layer of clouds blanketing the sky as far as the eye could see. From the looks of things, it wouldn't be long before the rain started. No doubt it would be one of those cold, miserable drizzles that were chilling enough to freeze a man's soul.

Mark turned away from the view, feeling more like 126 than his actual twenty-six. It was time to get ready to go to the office. He could put it off no longer.

It seemed to Mark that that was all he ever did anymore—work. He put in ten to twelve hours a day at his family's successful car-leasing business, then went to the gym at night to work out and try to burn off the angst that would not go away.

Jenny—

Hardly a day went by when he didn't think of her. It seemed she was always in his mind, and, despite all his attempts to put her from him, she remained in his heart.

"Damn." The word escaped Mark in a painful sigh, and he wondered if he would ever be free of Jenny.

He headed for the bathroom to shower. He had less than an hour to get downtown, and it was a forty-minute drive. Not that he hadn't made the trip in less. There had been days in the last six months when he'd driven it in as little as twenty-five minutes. A lot of other drivers hadn't been too pleased with the way he'd maneuvered his sleek, low-slung sports car through the traffic with swift, sure, rapid moves, but he hadn't cared. In fact, it seemed he hadn't cared about much lately.

Mark stripped and stepped into the shower. Beneath the soothing heat of the water, he flexed his broad shoulders, corded and sleek with muscles developed during all those workouts at the gym. The steady warm massage eased some of the tension from him, and after long minutes, Mark finally turned the shower off and got out. He dressed quickly in his designer suit, white shirt and power tie. He looked the successful young executive that he was.

His mother had always impressed upon him that image was everything. If you wanted to be successful, you had to look successful. Not that he had to struggle to succeed in business. Seton Leasing was already a successful company with a wonderful reputation. Mark's fortunes were secured for the rest of his life, thanks to his mother's wise investments and aggressive marketing of the business. If nothing else, his mother was an astute businesswoman.

Mark made it to the office in almost record time. He didn't care. He was there. The work was waiting for him.

"Good morning, Mr. Seton," called Joanne Neely, Mark's secretary for the last three years. Joanne was an efficient, hard-working widow of forty-two who was trying to raise two teenagers on her secretary's pay. She was defiantly cheerful, no matter what the situation, and always believed that everything would eventually turn out all right if you worked hard enough. Hardly a day went by that Mark didn't see her at lunch with a romance novel in hand. He teased her about her reading tastes, telling her she should be living her fantasies, not reading about them, but she invariably told him she'd had the love of her life once with her dead husband, and she doubted it could ever be so sweet again.

"You look as thunderous as the weather," Joanne remarked, seeing his serious, almost scowling expression. "Is something wrong? Do we have trouble today?"

Mark managed a slightly weary smile. "No. Everything is actually kind of peaceful."

His mother was out of town attending a business conference in Phoenix, and he was in charge until her return.

"Good. Peaceful is nice sometimes." She looked thoughtful for a moment. "Although I love this place when it gets exciting and busy, too."

"I don't think I've ever seen you less than happy," Mark remarked.

"It's easy to be miserable if you choose to be. I make a decision to be happy every day. I get up each morning and make up my mind that I'm going to try to see the good in everybody and the humor in every situation. Some days it isn't easy."

Mark gave her an affectionate smile. "You make it look easy."

"I guess I'm a better actress than I thought," she quipped, returning his smile.

Her heart went out to him as she watched him disappear into the inner sanctum of his walnut-paneled office. During the time she had worked for Mark, she had watched him grow from an inexperienced businessman fresh out of the university to one heck of a shrewd dealmaker. She had quietly looked on as he'd learned the business from his mother, and she had silently applauded him as he'd come to match Margo Seton in intelligent decision-making. Still, Joanne believed there was something about Mark—some hint of sadness in his eyes—that gave testimony to a hidden pain she suspected he kept shielded from the world. She prided herself on being able to read men pretty well, especially since she had her own two sons, seventeen and nineteen, to keep ahead of. She felt certain that something had happened to Mark in the past year to change him. Something had hardened him somehow, and she wondered about his private life. Certainly, his professional life had been a rousing success.

Mark strode to his desk and sorted through the messages Joanne had left there. He found nothing pressing, just the usual reminders of his appointments for the day. He had a meeting at ten with the advertising agency and lunch with Christine Barrett. He paused as he thought of the beautiful accountant who was "mother-approved." He grimaced as he thought of how his mother had plotted to get them together. At a charity ball two months before, she'd arranged for the Barrett family to sit at their table, seating the two of them side by side. Of course, he found Christine attractive. What was not to like about her? She was petite. Her hair was fashionably ash-blond. She was dressed immaculately in the most current fashion, and was well educated. She was a CPA. Christine was beautiful, smart and socially acceptable. The perfect potential mate for the Seton heir, but she wasn't—

Mark stopped and muttered a curse under his breath. Disgusted with himself and the train of his thoughts, he sat down at the desk and started to go through the paperwork. If he kept busy he would be all right. If he just kept busy—

The morning flew by, an endless round of phone calls and dictation.

It was 11:30 when Joanne knocked twice and opened the door. "Ms. Barrett called and said she would meet you at noon at the Rainbow Room."

Mark glanced at his watch and then slowly stood. The sun still hadn't made an appearance, and the grayness of the day colored his mood. Shrugging back into the suit coat he'd shed earlier, he started to leave the office.

"I should be back by one-thirty. I'll call you if there's been any delay."

He left the office building and emerged onto the rain-dampened streets of downtown. Skyscrapers towered above him. Traffic was snarled. People rushed by, hurried and harassed, their gazes downcast, their expressions unreadable. Mark paid little attention to his surroundings, and he didn't bother to ponder the mysteries of life. He had been living life one hour at a time for so long now that he saw little point in pondering the deeper meaning of his existence. If he had been called upon to espouse a theory of life, he supposed his current one would be that everything one did was really pointless, just a simple exercise in futility, killing time until there was no more time.

The Rainbow Room was crowded as Mark stepped inside, and he was welcomed immediately by the maitre d'.

"Good afternoon, Mr. Seton. Ms. Barrett is waiting for you at your usual table."

"Thank you, Thomas." He headed for the quiet table in the far corner. He ate at the restaurant regularly, often bringing business associates there to celebrate the closing of a deal.

Christine was wearing a vibrant yellow wool blazer over a black form-fitting dress. Tasteful gold earrings and a heavy gold chain completed the outfit. She looked up and smiled at him as he drew near.

"Christine, you look beautiful as always," Mark greeted her, kissing the cheek she offered him. He meant every word. She was a classic beauty. Mark knew she had once worked as a model before going into accounting.

"You are a charmer, Mark Seton, but I love it," she laughed lightly, very pleased by his compliment. She had taken even more care than usual with her hair and makeup today, and she'd made sure to wear the perfect outfit. She was out to impress him, and she wanted to do a good job.

As Mark took the chair across from her, a waiter appeared. They took the menus but set them aside while they spoke of all that had happened since their last date the weekend before. Mark listened as Christine went on about one of her clients and some complicated dealings with the IRS. She was an intelligent woman, sure to succeed at whatever she tried her hand at. He admired her and enjoyed her companionship.

After a while they placed their orders and were quickly served. Christine waited until they were just about done with the delicious fare before broaching the subject she'd been waiting to discuss with him.

"Daddy plans to go to the lodge this weekend, and we were wondering if you'd like to join us. I know how busy you are, but I'm sure we'd be able to find some time alone if you decided to come along."

The weekends were the times when Mark made the social scene. There was always some charity event that demanded an appearance, some function of importance he had to attend.

"Let me check the calendar and call you this evening," he answered, knowing an invitation from her father was a minor business coup, but stalling just enough to keep from committing himself before he'd thought it through. She had spoken of the two of them finding time alone. If she was ready to deepen their relationship, it might be best if he stayed away. He was not ready to commit to anyone. He was not ready to share the intimacy of his bed with anyone. He had remained celibate for over six months now, and he would remain so until he finally married—whenever that might be.

"I have a dinner meeting tonight, but I should be home by ten. Let me know and I'll tell my father." She changed the subject. "So, how is the work going with your mother away?"

"Very well. I've got meetings with the Devonshire people this week, and hopefully I can conclude the deal before she returns."

"That would be wonderful. She'd be so proud of you."

Mark thought of his mother, the beautiful

Margo, of her social astuteness and business cunning. Since his father's death ten years before, she had taken over Seton Leasing and had doubled the profits of the business. He doubted she would be proud of anything he did. Satisfied, maybe, but proud? He didn't think so.

As he thought about Christine's statement, he found himself wondering if he even cared if his mother was proud of him. Their relationship had grown strained during the past six months, and he'd been tempted to leave Seton Leasing more than once. Her iron will, however, had overruled him every time. Sometimes he truly regretted that he hadn't stood up to her, hadn't struck out on his own. And influencing all his feelings was the memory of Jenny—

"Mark? Is something wrong?" Christine was not an especially insightful person, but there was no mistaking the sudden darkening of his expression.

He glanced up sharply, as if dragged back to reality too abruptly. "No—sorry. I was just thinking about all the work I have waiting for me when I get back to the office." He managed a tight smile.

"I guess we'd both better be getting back, then." She rose and he followed her. "I'll hear from you soon about this weekend?"

"As soon as I know something, I'll call you."

"I'll be waiting." In her voice was a breathless invitation.

Mark heard it but refused to acknowledge it. They parted in front of the restaurant, Christine walking back to her office on the twelfth floor of a nearby high-rise, Mark striding toward his own plush suite at Seton Leasing Corporate Headquarters. He had almost reached the main entrance of Seton Tower when an impulse drove him to keep walking. Traffic was heavy, for it was still lunchtime, and he found himself dodging between trucks, cabs and cars as he made his way toward the park that was the central attraction downtown.

There were moments when he found spending time in the park calming, and today was one of those days. He needed to sit on a bench by the lake and stare out across the peaceful water, if only for a little while. He had just about made it to the crosswalk when the light changed and he was forced to wait for the walk signal. A bus moved before him, making its way slowly in the bumper-to-bumper flow.

He wasn't really paying attention.

He wasn't really looking.

But suddenly, there she was in the window of the bus.

Jenny—

Everything stopped in his mind. Sounds around him faded to nothingness. Mark stood frozen on that corner as the bus inched past him. He couldn't tear his gaze away. It was as if his soul thirsted for the sight of her. The world around him vanished—

There was only Jenny—

She was reading, her head bent, a look of concentration on her face. He stared at the sweet curve of her cheek, the lush tumble of her dark hair loose about her shoulders, and then he remembered how cold she had been when last they'd talked. Pain slashed at him, deep and real. He had never wanted to hurt her. He had loved her.

Jenny—

At that instant, almost as if she'd heard his deepest, innermost thoughts, Jenny looked up. Their gazes met. A look of shock flashed in her eyes.

Her name was on Mark's lips. He wanted to call out to her. To stop the bus.

But Jenny's expression hardened.

The traffic began to move.

The bus pulled away.

She was gone.

Mark stared after the ponderous vehicle. A part of him urged him to give chase, to run after the bus, to flag it down and claim Jenny as his own, but he fought it. Ignoring the strange looks of the pedestrians around him, he turned away from the park and headed back to the office.

He had work to do there.

And he would call Christine.

Jenny's heart was pounding as she tore her gaze away from Mark. She tried to calm herself. She hadn't expected to ever see him again, and it infuriated her that just one glimpse of him could affect her this way. She was still vulnerable where he was concerned, and she didn't want to be.

Jenny steeled herself against her betraying emotions. She had her baby to think about. Her baby was all that mattered. Mark was gone from her life and would never return, and she wanted it that way.

CHAPTER FOUR

Dorothy's meeting with the lawyer went as smoothly as could be expected. He was going to take care of things for her. She was still numb and barely functioning as she drove away from his office.

Dorothy did not want to go home, so she stopped at the grocery store. She lingered there for as long as she could, making small talk with a friendly clerk, until she knew she could avoid it no longer.

The drive was a short one, and then she was home.

Home—

The word echoed as hollowly in her mind as the sound of the door shutting on the empty house. She was there, and now she was really alone. She'd fought it for as long as she could, but there could be no more hiding from the truth.

What had happened last night had been real. It had not been a bad dream. Alan was gone. He really had left her for another woman—a younger woman.

Mechanically Dorothy went into the kitchen and made a pot of very strong coffee. A part of her would have preferred straight whiskey, but this was not the time to lose her composure and her control. She wouldn't give him that satisfaction. Later she would drown her sorrows, but right now she had to come to grips with what had happened.

Fear ate at her. What was she going to do? Alan had been her sole support for all these years. He had taken care of her since the day they married, and she in turn had taken care of him—or at least she'd thought she'd taken care of him. And yet he had left her for someone else—someone younger—prettier—

What would she do? She had always volunteered her services, never feeling the need to get a paying job; Alan had been blessed with a very successful career. Yet once they divorced, she would have to support herself, and she had no idea how.

The ache of terror and fear and confusion within her grew. She had not known that pain could be so great. How could Alan be such a liar? His actions refuted all he had professed to believe. Hadn't they taken vows before God that said "forsaking all others 'til death do us part"? Hadn't they sworn to "love and cherish one another"? What had happened? What had gone wrong?

She rose and walked slowly into the bathroom to stare at her reflection in the mirror. In the semi-shadowed darkness, Dorothy could still see the twenty-five-year-old beauty she'd been when she'd wed Alan all those years ago.

But then she turned on the light switch.

An old woman glared at her.

Despite the hair-coloring, use of Retin-A and carefully applied makeup, there could be no hiding the fact that she was not twenty-five anymore, and she never would be again.

A lone tear trickled from the corner of her eye as she studied the woman staring back at her in the mirror.

Was this what it meant to grow old?

To be abandoned by the man you'd loved for over thirty years?

Where was the justice in it?

Where was God?

A sob broke from her, and turning away from the painful sight of her own reflection, she ran blindly from the room and fell upon the bed, crying.

The dam had burst. It would be hours before the flood tide of misery quieted.

Joe got home early from work that afternoon to find Gail playing in the living room with Scott and Tara, their daughter Angie's children. Toys were strewn everywhere, but he didn't mind. In fact, he loved the happy confusion. The house had seemed empty ever since their youngest son,

Marty, had married and moved out several years before.

The house was not big, but what it lacked in space, it made up for in love. Peace and joy vibrated from every corner of the home. Pictures of family and friends adorned the walls, along with crayon drawings produced by the next generation of brilliant offspring.

"Evening, darlings," he called out as he came in through the kitchen.

"Hello, sweetheart! How was your day?" Gail asked, leaving the two five-year-olds to their own devices for a moment as she went to kiss him.

"Long and lonely. It's good to be home."

"Your supper's not quite ready," she admitted a little guiltily. "I got a bit carried away with the kids."

Joe laughed good-naturedly as he settled down in the living room, where he was immediately overrun by the two youngsters. Hugs and kisses were bounteous as they welcomed their grampa home from work, and then it grew quiet as he agreed to read them a story. Gail started fixing the meal.

"Will the kids be here long?"

"No. Angie said Buddy would be picking them up before seven, but we'll have time for dinner."

"Good. What're we having?"

"Hot dogs and chips."

He glanced at her quickly, surprised by the summer fare. Gail only shrugged.

40

"The kids said those were Grampa's favorite foods, and we wanted to please Grampa."

"I must have mentioned that to them last summer at the barbecue."

"Well, that's what you're getting. We'll be eating in about ten minutes."

They fell into their usual happy routine, Joe playing with the kids while Gail cooked. It was just like years before, when Angie and Marty had been at home. It felt good.

They said grace over the meal, then ate the picnic-style food, which tasted as good as any gourmet dining to Joe. When at last the grandkids had been picked up and Joe and Gail were alone, Joe remembered seeing Jenny that morning at church.

"Have you seen Jenny Emerson lately?"

"Not in the last few months. Why?"

Joe was quiet, wondering how to phrase the news.

At his hesitation, Gail knew something was troubling him and asked quickly, "Is she all right?"

"I'm not sure."

"What do you mean?"

"Well, I saw her this morning at Mass."

"And?"

"And she's pregnant."

Gail only stared at him in confusion. "But she isn't married, is she?"

Joe couldn't help smiling slightly at her observation. "Things are a little different these days, I'm afraid."

Gail flushed. "Well, they shouldn't be. No, I didn't know about her condition. No one's said a word. Is she far along?"

"Very. Eighth or ninth month, if I'm any judge from remembering what you looked like."

"She was with a very nice young man last summer at the festival. Remember that boy?" She was frowning as she tried to conjure up his face and name. "Mark was his first name, I think."

"Yes. That's it—Mark, Mark Seton. Didn't he work for Seton Leasing?"

"Yes, he did. I think his family owns it." She could see the couple clearly in her mind's eye now, holding hands as they'd wandered through the booths of crafts and games at the parish picnic on the church grounds. They had seemed so happy— so much in love. "I thought surely they were going to get married. He was looking at her as if he loved her more than life itself."

"I know." Joe remembered, too.

"Do you suppose she's all right? Do you think she needs anything?" Gail was concerned.

"I could ask Father, but I know it's really none of my business."

"Sometimes to make things better for others, we have to make it our business," Gail said softly, knowing that many people had too much pride to ask for help. "Check with Father. He'll know what to do."

"I'll talk with him in the morning."

* * *

Jenny curled up in bed and hugged her pillow to her. She felt about five years old, but she knew she was a woman full-grown. She wanted to be a little girl again, to have her mother hug her and rock her and tell her everything would be all right. But her mother had died three years before and her father soon after.

She was alone.

Funny how sometimes life could be really wonderful, and how, when you were living the good times, you thought they'd last forever.

Funny how they never did last forever.

She closed her eyes as her baby moved within her. An overwhelming sense of love filled her. This was her child.

At lunch today, Jenny had left the office and gone to one of the church-sponsored centers that helped place newborns for adoption. Donna, her best friend at work, had recommended the place to her. She had not considered the option before, but now that the baby's birth was so near, there was no hiding from reality anymore. She had to make the right decision.

It had been a very emotional meeting for Jenny. Sister Mary Catherine, an ageless woman with soft brown eyes that seemed to look into the depths of Jenny's soul, had been the one to interview her. The good sister had been gentle yet direct in her questioning, drawing out Jenny's whole story with infinite patience and concern. Under her guidance and thoughtfully worded inquiries,

Jenny had done a lot of soul-searching. She had faced her dilemma head-on and had discussed every possibility. Still, she had not been able to make up her mind.

Jenny loved her unborn child, but would she be doing the right thing to try to raise her son or daughter alone? Or would the child be better off with an adoptive family who could give it everything it needed—a mother and father who loved it, a secure home and no financial worries?

"I went to Mass this morning," she had told Sister Mary Catherine as she was pulling on her coat to leave after more than an hour in conference.

The sister had beamed at this news. "Of all the things you could do right now to help yourself and your child, prayer is the most important. I can guide you in some ways, but only God can show you the path that is right for you. Listen with all your heart. Watch carefully for the answer to your prayers. Sometimes prayers are answered in ways so completely foreign to us, and yet so perfect, that it is hard for us to believe such could happen."

"Do you really think God is listening to me?" Jenny had asked the woman of faith, wondering how the sister could be so sure, so confident. "It seems as if I've been talking to Him and talking to Him and He never answers."

Sister Mary Catherine had smiled gently. "He's listening. It's just that sometimes what He's got planned for us takes a little while to arrange. Trust in God's love. He is always there, just out of sight, watching over you."

Jenny's eyes had filled with tears as she'd hugged the dear woman. "Thank you."

Sister Mary Catherine had hugged her back. "You take care of yourself, Jenny Emerson. I'll wait to hear from you. Let me know whatever you decide."

"I will. I promise."

She had left the facility, calmed by the sister's prayerful concern, yet still profoundly troubled about the future she was facing alone.

And then she'd seen Mark through the bus window.

The shock was still with her now. She hadn't imagined that seeing him again would jar her so deeply. Somehow she'd managed to get through the rest of the day at work, but now she was haunted by her memories of him—of the love they'd shared—of the joy she'd known in his arms.

Jenny pushed the memories from her mind. What she'd believed was real had all been a lie. He hadn't loved her. She had meant nothing to him. They were through. She was a woman now, no longer an innocent romantic. And she would soon be a mother. Her baby was all that mattered.

But what was she going to do?

Panic filled her. Was there no one she could turn to and rely on?

There was no one—except God.

Jenny began to pray silently, fervently, begging for guidance, begging for a miracle to help her make her decision, begging for some sign that she had done the right thing in not having an abortion.

The baby kicked.

Jenny cried.

"Hey, baby, I made it!" Claire said as she rushed into the apartment that night.

"I was hoping you would. I missed you today," Darrell admitted as he went to her. He had slept for a while, watched TV for a while and then had grown bored, locked alone in the small apartment. When Claire came through the door, she brightened his life like the sun coming through the clouds after a long, dreary rain.

"How much?" she teased as she put the bag of fast-food burgers on the counter and went into his arms.

His kiss was warm and welcoming, and they settled on the sofa to share the meal she'd brought home.

"What did you do all day?"

"I was lazy. All I did was sleep." His answer was easy, untroubled. "You work hard?"

"You'd better believe it. The doctor's office was crowded. Everybody's got the flu or something. We didn't quit until half an hour ago."

They fell silent as they ate, watching TV. Seven-thirty came far too soon for Darrell. As much as he would have liked to linger with Claire, he couldn't be late for his job. Stan Schmidt, his parole officer, had helped him get the position, and he was not about to let the man down.

"I gotta go." He stood regretfully and left her to pull on a lightweight jacket and dark baseball cap.

"Why are you wearing that hat? And that jacket isn't gonna keep you warm—it's cold tonight."

He shrugged, not wanting to wear the coat he'd had on last night. True, it was his only warm coat, but he feared that someone might identify him by it. He had to change his look. It was one of the few chances he had.

"You ever think about leaving the city?" he asked as he put his hand on the doorknob and stopped to glance back at her.

"All the time, sugar, and especially on nights like this."

"Let's go south, then. Someplace warmer—Mississippi, Louisiana, Texas." He wanted to run away as far and as fast as he could. He wanted to escape this place and its stranglehold on him. He wanted to save himself and the life he'd been try-ing to rebuild with Claire.

She smiled. "We'll leave first thing in the morning as soon as you get off work."

For an instant, Darrell almost believed her and his spirits soared. Then, just as quickly, he real-ized she was teasing. "I'm ready to leave."

"I know it, but we both know you can't go any-where, sweetheart," she said, "not for another twenty-eight months. Once you're off parole, I'll quit my job and we can go wherever you want. We'll start over fresh someplace new."

"You promise?"

"I promise, but it sure would be nice to head south now, when the weather's cold and miserable here."

Darrell opened the door and the chill of the hall hit him. He shivered in spite of himself. "Hold on to that thought. Three years from now, we'll be basking in the sunshine."

"I'm ready, but until then I'll be waiting right here for you."

Darrell closed and locked the door behind him and started off to his job on the docks. He was due to see Stan Schmidt soon, and he wondered if there was any way he could leave town without getting in trouble. As long as the parole office knew where to find him, he didn't see a problem. He figured it was at least worth asking. The worst Schmidt could say was no.

Starting off down the street toward the bus stop, Darrell tried to ignore the bite of the December cold through the thin jacket. It was going to be a long night.

CHAPTER FIVE
DAY TWO

Lord Have Mercy. . .

Darrell was so busy all night that he didn't have time to think about the cold. In fact, he was working so hard that a couple of times he broke into a sweat. He did not complain. As quitting time edged ever closer, he kept wondering which way he should go home. He had no intention of cutting down that same side street he had traveled yesterday. He started slowly from the building.

"Miller!"

At Gary Burke's call, Darrell stopped short, wondering what his co-worker wanted. He'd finished his job and knew he hadn't screwed up in any way. "Yeah. What d'ya want?"

"You want a ride as far as Grand?" the older man offered.

"Thanks!" He was surprised by the invitation, but quickly accepted. A ride was just what he needed.

"It gets damned cold waiting for the buses. I know. I did it before I saved up enough to buy a car."

They piled into Burke's beat-up Maverick. It was old, real old, and it was ugly, but it ran like a top and the heater worked just fine. Darrell wouldn't have been happier in a limo. They made small talk as Burke maneuvered through the city streets.

"Schmidt your parole officer?" Burke asked.

"How'd you know?"

"I did my share of time, too. Schmidt's an all-right guy. He'll do what he can for you. You just have to do what you can for yourself."

"I'm trying."

"I know. I heard the boss talking, and he was saying that you're doing a good job."

Darrell glanced at him in surprise. Seldom in his life had he been praised for anything. "Thanks for telling me."

"No problem."

"So what were you in for?"

"A little mistake in judgment in my youth," Gary said. "Thought I could get money the easy way . . . by ripping off a liquor store."

"You got caught?"

"First try. Damn, I was stupid. I know better now, though. Been clean for seventeen years. There's only one way to do it when you're all alone and feel like the world's against you."

Darrell didn't ask, but his expression evinced curiosity.

"Religion. You gotta get religion or none of this makes any sense." Burke gestured to the world around them.

"You ain't one of them holy rollers, are you?" Darrell sneered.

Gary shot him a censuring look. "There's nothing wrong with 'holy rollers,' as you call them. They ain't out robbing liquor stores and shooting people, are they?" He took Darrell's silence as assent. "What I'm telling you, Darrell, is that you look like a good man. You look like you got brains. So use 'em. You can rise above this. I know you can, but it takes more strength than what we got. That's why you need Jesus."

"Yeah, yeah," he said, just trying to get Gary to shut up.

"I ain't trying to convert you or anything. I'm just telling you what worked for me. Think about it, all right?"

"Sure."

"Here you go," Burke said as he pulled to the curb at Grand.

"Thanks for the lift. I appreciate it." The street was deserted as Darrell climbed out.

"Any time. See you tonight."

Darrell locked and shut the door and watched as Burke drove off. He wasn't quite sure what to make of their conversation.

The icy wind hit Darrell like a freight train. He shoved his hands deep in his pockets as he glanced up the street and saw someone going up the steps and into Our Lady. As the door opened, a ray of light shone, but when the door closed, all was dark again. He thought of the Mass and of the priest who'd spoken to him the night before. He tried to remember his name and couldn't.

Darrell turned away, wanting to go home. It was then that Our Lady's bell tolled the half hour. He glanced back and saw her there, waiting patiently, questioning his hesitation, inviting him to come in. He gave his head a shake, wondering where the thoughts were coming from, even as he headed toward the church.

"What the hel. . . . heck," he amended his thought quickly. He'd made it safely through a whole day and had gotten an unexpected ride this morning. Maybe there was something to this God stuff.

He went in.

Everything looked much the same as it had the day before. It seemed that many of the same people were there, sitting in the same pews as yesterday—the pregnant girl near the back like him, the tall, older woman closer to the front, the one man off to the side. There were others—several couples and a lone man and lone woman. In all, maybe fifteen people were there, counting the priest. Not very many, he mused, considering the size of the church. He wondered why nobody else was there. He wondered, too, why these people were. This was the second day in a row for some of them. He wondered why they kept coming.

Darrell hadn't paid much attention to the Catholic prayers the day before, but now he found himself listening. He even picked up a missalette to try to keep track.

"I confess to almighty God, and to you, my brothers and sisters, that I have sinned through my own fault, in my thoughts and in my words, in what I have done, and in what I have failed to do; and I ask Blessed Mary, ever virgin, all the angels and saints, and you, my brothers and sisters, to pray for me to the Lord our God," the congregation recited the penitential rite.

In what I have done and what I have failed to do. The words stung Darrell. He knew what he'd done and he knew what he'd failed to do, and his actions were keeping him alive. He refused to feel guilty about his decision. There were times in a man's life when running and keeping his mouth shut were more important than doing the right thing—no matter what Burke or the Catholics said.

When at last the time came for Communion, Darrell once again slipped quietly away. The street was busier this morning, but he saw nothing threatening, no car that looked like it was trolling the neighborhood in search of someone. Still, he did not feel comfortable enough with his change-of-clothes disguise to take the main drags. He went down the passageway again, half expecting the old priest to be waiting for him. He felt strangely disappointed when he didn't see him.

Darrell hurried home by way of back streets again.

* * *

After leaving Mass, Jenny went to the garage to pick up her car, then drove straight to work at the television station. She entered the office where the news writers worked to find Donna already there, waiting for her. That was very unusual. Donna was no early bird, and she was often the last one to arrive. But this morning, she was already sitting in the office, looking none the worse for her early appearance. Her blond hair was done up in a smooth, chic style. Her makeup was perfect, as always, and the suit she wore was sophisticated and professional. Donna was respected by all at the station for her business savvy and for her ability to work through difficulties without panic. There was a calmness, a serenity, about her that inspired trust. They had become friends when Jenny had come to work at the station right out of college two years before.

"How did it go?" Donna asked. She'd been worrying about Jenny since her friend had left yesterday to go to the adoption center. She'd missed seeing her in the afternoon and had even called her at home last night to find out how things had gone, but had gotten no answer.

"You were right. They were extraordinarily nice at the center. I don't think I've ever met a more gentle woman than Sister Mary Catherine."

"Did the visit help?"

Jenny's carefully schooled expression faltered a little. "We talked for a long time. She helped me understand a lot of things about myself and about my situation."

"And?"

"And I still don't know what I'm going to do."

Donna couldn't stop herself from going to Jenny and giving her a hug. "It's going to work out. I'm sure of it."

"You're a lot more confident than I am," Jenny sighed, her voice shaky.

"No, I just know you. You're strong. You could have taken the easy way out. You could have had an abortion and been done with all this months ago, but you didn't."

"I couldn't kill my baby . . . Mark's baby . . ." Her voice was hoarse, and there was heartfelt agony in her dark-eyed gaze.

Donna winced slightly at Jenny's words. "I know. You're brave and kind, and if you decide to have this child and raise it yourself, you'll do a fine job."

"I'll try. That's for sure." She managed a wavering smile, her friend's compliment touching her deeply. "Now, enough about me or you'll have me crying in another minute. Let's get to work. How's the world looking today?"

"You had to ask? Ugly as usual."

They both sighed as they separated to go to their desks.

Paige Stewart sat at her desk in the back office of Total Elegance Boutique, frowning. The invoices spread out before her did not lie. Try as she might, there was no avoiding the truth. She needed help.

Her slender shoulders slumped as she stared down at the papers. The business had seemed to be going smoothly since she'd taken Linda Mason on as partner six months before. Things had seemed to be working out.

And seemed *was the key word in that sentence*, Paige thought.

Total Elegance Boutique, Paige's dream since she'd been old enough to understand and fall in love with fashion, had taken every penny she had and three years' worth of twenty-hour workdays to get on its feet. The small, exclusive shop had done reasonably well until the economy had tightened up about a year ago. That was when she'd invited Linda to become a partner. The other woman had provided some of the capital Paige needed to keep the right kind of merchandise in the store until business picked up. And business was picking up. The trouble was, Linda had pulled out.

Unexpectedly.

Unannounced.

Two weeks before, Linda had just pulled the plug on their business relationship and flown off to Cancún to elope with some man she barely knew.

Paige sighed out loud. She hoped Linda was happy. She didn't wish her any ill. She just wanted Total Elegance to stay afloat, and for the life of her, she didn't know how she was going to do it. Her credit was maxed out, and though her husband, Rick, had a good job, he didn't make enough to bankroll the store.

The prospects did not look good. She said a small prayer that she'd find a way out of her financial difficulties.

"Good morning!"

Paige heard Dorothy Pennington's greeting and smiled. Dorothy was one of the classiest women she knew, and if nothing else could brighten up her day, Dorothy could. She always managed to see the good side of every situation. Paige firmly believed that ability was a gift from God, for try as she might, she could find nothing to be happy about in her current situation. In less than two months, if she didn't come up with an injection of funds, Total Elegance was going to cease to exist.

Her dream would be gone.

Her chance to prove herself would have failed.

Determined to put on a happy face for Dorothy, Paige shoved the papers back in the file folder and left the office to wait on her. She'd let all the sales help go except for the one part-time person who worked evenings. The weight of responsibility was heavy this day.

"Good morning, Dorothy," Paige called as she emerged from the backroom. "What brings you out so early today?"

Total Elegance was known for its sophisticated atmosphere. The shop was done in shades of soft mauve and off-white, with mirrors everywhere to enhance the lighting and better display the merchandise.

Racks of rainbow-hued gowns, dressy business clothes, bejeweled sweaters and sparkling accessories filled the boutique. It was a clothes lover's haven. A chic place. Coffee, mints and cookies were always offered, and an overstuffed sofa with end tables provided a comfortable place to sit and talk. The atmosphere was sleek, modern and totally elegant, as its name promised.

Dorothy glanced up from where she was looking through a rack of blazers to see the owner coming her way. She looked beautiful as always. "Hi, Paige. I couldn't stay away, and besides, I was hoping you'd be here."

"Where else would I be?" she laughed. "Total Elegance is my life."

"I envy you that. What a wonderful place this would be to work in." Dorothy wished she had something to do besides charity work. It was fulfilling and she did enjoy it, but now . . . She was going to have to get a job. A happy thought formed—maybe Paige would hire her. A bud of excitement grew within her. It was her first bit of hope since this mess started. Trouble was, she hadn't worked in years, and she wondered how to go about asking for a job.

"I do love it. Sometimes too much," Paige replied, trying to hide the note of sadness in her voice. If she lost Total Elegance, she'd be lost. "So, where are you and your wonderful husband jetting off to now?"

Paige knew that Dorothy and Alan traveled a lot, and she was always eager to help put together a new wardrobe. The sudden change in Dorothy's expression surprised Paige.

"Dorothy, what is it? What's wrong?"

Dorothy had been almost relaxed, but at the mention of Alan, all the pain returned. "There's something wrong, all right." Bitterness sounded clearly in her voice.

"What? Can you talk about it?"

"I can talk about it, but it won't change anything." Dorothy turned to face her friend and lifted her troubled gaze to hers. "Alan has left me, Paige."

Paige almost felt as if she'd been struck a physical blow. "What? You're kidding."

"I wish I were." Her mouth twisted as her composure threatened to break.

"I'm so sorry. What happened?"

"I don't know," Dorothy answered with a slight lift of her shoulders. "I thought everything was fine. I thought we were happy. I was wrong."

"Oh, Dorothy." Paige could see how much her friend was suffering. She went to her and gave her a warm hug. She'd always thought of Dorothy as a strong woman, but suddenly she felt very fragile in her arms.

"I haven't even gathered up the courage to tell David and Carol yet," Dorothy went on, mentioning her children.

"When did all this happen?"

"Yesterday." Dorothy allowed herself a moment

to take comfort in Paige's caring, then drew away. It wouldn't do to break down completely. "I'm sorry."

"For what? There's nothing for you to be sorry for," Paige replied gently. "Is there anything I can do? Any way I can help?"

"Can you give me a job? I'm going to have to go to work once the lawyers are through, and there's no place I'd rather work than here, with you."

Paige saw the hope in her friend's eyes and wanted with all her heart to tell her yes, but there was no way she could do it. She hadn't drawn a salary for herself in all the years the store had been open, and now, after losing her partner, she couldn't take on any help. "There's nothing I'd like more than to work with you, too, but I can't do it right now. Things are not the greatest around here. I've been running the shop by my-self with only some part-time help at night."

"I see," Dorothy said slowly. She was certain Paige was turning her down because she was old and nobody wanted her. She couldn't even get hired as a salesclerk. She managed a smile, want-ing to put Paige at ease.

"I wish I could help you." Paige said. "I tell you what. If I hear of any stores around here that might be hiring, I'll let you know."

"Thanks."

"You want some coffee?"

"I'd love some."

Paige went to pour her a cup so they could set-tle in for a nice visit, but as she returned, another customer entered the store. They were unable to talk intimately anymore.

Dorothy busied herself for a while, bought a few things for her daughter and then left. It was still before noon, and she didn't quite know what to do with herself.

She supposed she should get in touch with her son and daughter. They certainly deserved to know what was going on, but she was still so filled with anger at Alan, she didn't want to speak of the divorce yet. She would tell them eventually. There really could be no avoiding it. But later.

CHAPTER SIX

Alan Pennington stretched out on the bed in the hotel, his smile one of a sated, happy man. Water was running in the shower where Tina had just gone to freshen up before they went back to work. He had often wondered what it would be like to sneak out at lunch to make love, and now he knew. It was exciting—more exciting than he'd ever imagined.

They had been rushed.

They had been hot.

They had been ready.

It had been great.

His smile broadened. He could still do it.

Years ago, with Dorothy—

"Damn!" he swore under his breath, wondering why he'd thought of her right now. Sure, they'd had a good sex life years ago when first married, but this thing with Tina . . . this was different.

Being with a twenty-eight-year-old made him feel young and vital and alive. Wanting to push all thoughts of Dorothy from his mind, he got up and padded into the bathroom.

Tina let out a shriek as the shower stall door opened and Alan stepped inside with her.

"I missed you," he murmured. He took her by the waist and pulled her against him. She was young and firm and sleekened by the water, and he was instantly aroused. His mouth sought hers.

Tina returned his kiss with abandon. She could hardly believe it! Alan had really left his wife for her! The knowledge filled her with a great sense of power and excitement. She leaned against him, teasing him.

"Tina. . ." he whispered huskily.

They came together in fiery, forbidden passion.

A short time later, Tina gave a soft laugh and slipped from his arms. "I'll bet you've never had such a productive lunch hour in all your years at Warson-Freeman."

"Not that I can remember. And I certainly would remember any lunches like this one." Alan grinned at her and reached for her again.

Tina eluded him this time. "Oh, no. I have some work that has to be done this afternoon. We'd better hurry back. I'll bet our hour is almost over."

"I'd prefer to spend the rest of the afternoon in bed with you," he answered.

"I have an appointment with a client at one-thirty, but I might be able to come up to your office around three," she told him with a hint of promise in her voice.

A mental image of taking her there in his office sent a jolt of desire pounding through him again. It surprised him with its power. He wondered if he could possibly make love to her again. He smiled at the prospect of proving himself once more.

"I'll see what I can do, but call me first."

"Why? Don't you like surprises? It would be fun knowing your secretary was sitting right outside the door, wouldn't it?"

The heat within him grew at the illicitness of her suggestion. "Behave yourself."

"Why? You don't really want me to, do you?"

"If I'm in a meeting at three, there's always later . . . after hours." He was already looking forward to getting off work. Funny, work used to be the thing he enjoyed most, making deals, power lunches, but now, since Tina, he'd rather spend every moment with her.

Alan drew her to him and kissed her. It was deep and passionate, but they both knew it had to end. They were taking a big enough risk as it was, sneaking off like this.

"Later," she murmured as she turned off the water and reached out of the stall to get towels.

Alan took hers from her and dried her. Each stroke of the thick, soft towel was a promise of the pleasure to come later in the day. A short time later, they left the hotel separately. They were only a few minutes late getting back to work.

Alan had great difficulty concentrating on the meeting that began at 2:45 and lasted until almost 4:00.

Joe was due to go to a Men's Club meeting at church that night, so he left home half an hour early to have time to talk with Father Beck. As usual, the priest was mingling with those coming into the parish hall, greeting each new arrival and exchanging pleasantries. He was a popular man, having been the pastor at Our Lady for over six years. Joe considered Father Beck a good friend. Father Beck always knew he could count on Joe, and Joe always knew he could count on Father Beck. That's why he was pretty certain he could find some way to do something nice for Jenny Emerson, to help her out if she needed anything.

"How are you doing, Father?" Joe asked, going to stand with him near the back of the church.

"I'm fine, Joe, just fine, but I've got a feeling from the look in your eyes that I'm not going to be fine for long," the priest quipped.

"I don't know what you mean," Joe replied, pretending innocence, when he knew darn well that the holy man could read him like a book.

"You're up to something, Joe Myers, and I'll bet I'm about to find out what."

"Well, there is one small favor I wanted to ask you . . ."

"I knew it. Here it comes. Whenever you get that gleam in your eye, no one is safe within the parish boundaries."

"And that's bad?"

"Well . . ." Father Beck thought of some of Joe's inspired schemes for fund-raising. "I'll never forget the time you talked me into sitting in the dunking booth at the summer picnic."

It had been a very long, very wet day for him.

"We raised a lot of money for the parish with that dunking booth," Joe protested.

"I know, but it wasn't fair that you brought in the Little League pitchers to practice on me."

Joe grinned. "Ah, but think of all the good uses we put that money to—and you did stay cool all day."

"And what about the time you secretly persuaded the quilters to sew my likeness into one of their quilts for the Fall Quilt Social?"

"I thought it looked just like you." Joe looked a little sheepish. "And it was the highest-priced one sold that day."

"Only because my mother bought it," he growled.

"Bless her heart. It was sweet of her to come to the social and be so generous."

"And then there was the school auction." Father Beck gave Joe a stern look.

"You haven't forgotten that one yet?"

"How could I forget it?"

"I had no idea that the eighth graders had saved up that much money."

"I was their slave for a day!"

"Now, really, Father, was it that bad?"

"Have you ever taken a school bus full of

thirteen-year-olds to the drive-thru at McDonald's?"

"Well, no."

"I rest my case." He fought to keep from smiling at the memory.

"But they did pay over a hundred fifty bucks for your services, and it went to a good cause."

"I give up, Joe. You win. What are you planning for me now?"

"I'm not planning anything," he answered, turning more serious at the thought of young Jenny. He had seen her again that morning, and she'd looked tired and scared and more than a little lost. He knew it might be his imagination, but he didn't think so. "I just wanted to talk to you about Jenny Emerson."

"Oh?"

"She's been at six-thirty Mass the last couple of mornings, and I just wondered how she was doing. Is there anything she needs?"

"I haven't talked to her in a while."

"She's pregnant."

"Yes, I believe she's due to have the baby soon."

"Does she have family left here in town? I know her parents passed away a few years ago."

"There's no other family I know of."

"What about her boyfriend? Gail and I met him last summer, but we haven't seen him around lately."

"There's really not much I can tell you, Joe," Father Beck answered. He had spoken with Jenny some months before when she'd come to him in desperation, and he had counseled her then. She hadn't been back to see him privately since, but he realized she'd made the right decision about having her baby; she knew he would do all he could if she needed any help.

"I suppose the best thing I can do is talk to her myself," Joe said.

"It couldn't hurt. We can all use good friends."

"So I'm your friend?" Joe asked, fishing for a compliment.

"Joe, you liven up my life here at Our Lady so much, I don't know what I'd do without you."

"I feel the same way about you, Father." He laughed, and then added more seriously, "I'll see what I can do to help Jenny."

"If she needs anything, anything at all, just let me know. We have all kinds of resources we can call upon."

"I will. I'll speak to her tomorrow morning."

It was after ten. Dorothy sat alone in her darkened living room. She needed to call her children and tell them what had happened, but somehow she couldn't summon the strength. She stared at the phone on the table next to her and at the bottle of prescription pain killers sitting next to it. The pills were potent. She knew that. The doctor had given them to her the year before when she'd had surgery.

Dorothy picked up the bottle and read the directions. *Take two for the relief of pain. Do not take more than 8 in a 24-hour period. Do not operate machinery. Do not drink liquor.*

She managed a weary smile. It said they relieved pain, but that was physical pain, not emotional. She was reasonably sure, however, that if she took them all at one time, she wouldn't have another care in this miserable world.

Suicide—

If she ended it all right here and now, she wouldn't have to deal with any of her problems.

Alan didn't want her—

She couldn't get a job—

No one cared about her—

She was alone.

So very alone.

Dorothy turned the bottle mindlessly in her hand.

She had never in her entire life imagined she would face a moment like this.

"Oh, God," she choked out loud when she realized the direction of her thoughts. She threw the pills across the room, outraged with herself for even considering taking her own life.

What was she thinking?

Life was precious.

She grew increasingly furious with herself and with Alan.

Alan wasn't worth it. He wasn't worth one more tear.

A quieting inner strength filled Dorothy, pushing away all the doubts and sorrows that had haunted her every moment since their last conversation. It was time her children learned the truth.

Dorothy turned on the light. She picked up the phone and dialed her son's number. David was the eldest. She would tell him first. And after she'd talked with the children, she would get on with the rest of her life.

CHAPTER SEVEN
DAY THREE

Lord, Hear Our Prayer . . .

The alarm went off and Jenny groaned. The baby had been active all night, and there had been no getting comfortable. She was tempted to skip Mass that morning and stay in bed the extra hour. It would have been easy to give in and just lie there, but she forced herself to get up. She needed to leave. The time she spent at church was the only peace in her life right now.

Jenny was moving slowly as she got ready. It didn't surprise her that she needed extra makeup this morning to cover the dark circles under her eyes. She sighed as she left the bathroom and went down the hall to the stairs.

Jenny had made it about halfway down the steps to the foyer when she was suddenly overcome by a wave of dizziness. Unsteady, she made a grab for the hand railing, but she didn't react quickly enough. She lost her balance.

"Oh, God—!" she cried out as terror filled her.

Jenny fell down the remaining steps, landing heavily at the foot of the staircase. She lay unmoving for a moment and was fighting to catch her breath when a sudden violent pain wracked her. There was no blood and her water hadn't broken, but Jenny was still terrified that the baby might have been hurt in the fall. She struggled to her feet and made her way into the kitchen to the phone to call Donna.

"Hello?" Donna said in a sleepy voice.

"It's me, Donna. Can you get over here quick?"

"Why? What's wrong?" Donna was immediately wide awake at the sound of her friend's distress.

"I fell—"

"Did you call 911?"

"No. I'm not bleeding or anything, but I'm scared."

"I'll be right over. Go lie down until I get there."

"Thanks."

"Hey, that's what friends are for," Donna reassured her.

Relieved that Donna would soon be with her, Jenny lay down on the sofa to wait. The pain had gone, but the fear that the baby had been injured remained.

Donna broke speed records getting dressed and out of the house. She raced to Jenny's and hurried up to the front porch to ring the doorbell. She peeked in a window worriedly and was relieved when she saw her friend making her way slowly to the door.

"How are you?" Donna asked, rushing inside to take Jenny's arm and help her back to sit on the sofa. "What happened? How did you fall?"

"I was just coming downstairs and I got real dizzy."

"We're going to St. Luke's Hospital," she ordered in a tone that brooked no argument. Jenny looked pale, and Donna wanted to make sure she was all right.

Jenny didn't argue. She just got her purse.

"Let me help you," Donna offered, putting a supportive arm around her.

"Thanks."

They made their way to Donna's car.

Jenny had to admit to herself that she was glad for Donna's help. After what had happened earlier, she didn't want to risk falling again.

"Are you in any pain?" Donna asked as she opened the car door for her.

"No, not right now."

"Good. Just relax. I'll have you at St. Luke's in a few minutes." Donna hurried around to get in on her side, and they drove off quickly.

Jenny looked out the car window, and in the distance she could see Our Lady's steeple silhouetted against the pale, early morning sky. Silently she offered up a prayer for her baby's health.

* * *

"And forgive us our trespasses as we forgive those who trespass against us . . ." Father Walters led the recitation of the Our Father during Mass.

Dorothy recited the prayer and wondered if she would ever be able to find forgiveness in her heart. At this moment, she doubted it, even though Jesus had commanded that we should forgive seventy times seven.

Dorothy drew a deep breath and prayed even harder for peace in her life. She didn't know how long it would take, but she would find a way to go on. Certainly, the fury she was feeling now was easier to deal with than the despair that had nearly destroyed her earlier. She would never let Alan know how deeply his selfishness had hurt her. Never again would she give him that power over her.

"And lead us not into temptation, but deliver us from evil," Darrell recited fervently but quietly. He didn't know any of the other prayers the Catholics said during Mass, but he did know the Our Father. If ever he'd needed that prayer, it was now, for he definitely needed God's protection from evil. He'd made it to the church safely again this morning, and he'd been giving silent thanks ever since he'd entered the haven.

Darrell lifted his gaze to the older priest at the altar. When he'd come inside to find that he was the one saying Mass today, he'd actually been glad. Something about the man conveyed a sense of peace.

His gaze rose higher to study the crucifix over the altar, and Burke's words of the day before eerily slipped into his thoughts: *That's why you need Jesus.*

Darrell gave a slight, disbelieving shake of his head, trying to understand the thinking of a man who would offer himself up for the sins of the world. Not that it seemed Jesus's sacrifice had done much good. The world was still a miserable place as far as Darrell could tell.

Darrell usually left at Communion time, but today, drawn by the older priest's presence, he remained in his pew. He wasn't quite sure why, he just wasn't ready to leave yet.

"Mass is ended. Let us go in peace to love and serve the Lord," Father Walters pronounced.

"Thanks be to God."

Father Walters left the altar and walked down the aisle. For a moment as he passed Darrell, their gazes met. The priest nodded slightly in recognition before continuing on to the vestibule.

Darrell lingered, letting other parishioners go before leaving his pew. He didn't escape by the side door this morning, but instead followed the priest to the welcome area. He stood back, quietly watching until the others had greeted the priest and moved on.

"Good morning," Father Walters said.

"Morning." Darrell spoke more quietly than usual. He'd never had a conversation with a priest before and he was uneasy.

"It's good to see you again."

"You remember me?"

77

Father Walters nodded. "I saw you the other morning in the walkway."

"That was me."

"Are you new to the parish?"

"You could say that," Darrell hedged.

"Well, welcome to Our Lady, Mr.—?"

"Miller. I'm Darrell Miller."

"Mr. Miller, it's nice to meet you."

"Thanks," he replied, not sure what else to say.

"Do you need to talk?" Father Walters asked, sensing his uneasiness.

A part of Darrell wanted to slip away, but the genuine concern he saw in the priest's eyes kept him there. "You got time?"

"Always." Father Walters had noticed that Darrell hadn't gone to Communion, so he suggested, "Has it been long since your last confession? Do you want to go in the confessional?"

"I'm not Catholic," Darrell said quickly.

"Oh." Father Walters was surprised. "All right then, we can go back inside and sit in the church if you want."

"Is there someplace more private?" he asked, looking around a bit nervously. The church was so open, and several other people had stayed on to pray. He didn't want to risk anyone overhearing what he was about to say.

"Come with me." Father Walters led Darrell into a small room off the welcome area and closed the door behind them. "Have a seat," he suggested, motioning toward the table and chairs. "How can I help you?"

Darrell sat down, feeling definitely ill at ease. He didn't calm down until he focused on a picture hanging on the wall. It depicted Jesus knocking on a door. Darrell stared at it for a moment, then frowned.

"What's wrong?"

"That picture—there's no doorknob on the door."

"Exactly. It's very perceptive of you to notice. A lot of people don't," Father Walters said with a smile. "It's symbolic. The door has to be opened to Jesus from within. Just as we have to open our hearts and souls to Him. We have to invite Him into our lives."

Darrell looked over at the priest, still feeling uncomfortable and not quite sure of what he was doing. "I need to talk—"

"Go on."

He glanced toward the door, then back at Father Walters. "I'm an ex-con. I've been trying to stay out of trouble, but a few nights ago I saw something I wasn't supposed to see."

The priest remained silent, listening, waiting.

"There was a shooting about six blocks over— a drive-by. I saw the whole thing. A guy was killed."

"Did you go to the police?"

"Hell, no!" Darrell blurted out. Then he quickly apologized, "Sorry, Father."

"Why not? You can identify the killers. They should be brought to justice."

Darrell fixed the religious man with a cold-eyed glare. "I'm in no hurry to die."

"The police have ways to protect witnesses."

Darrell snorted derisively. "I'm an ex-con. They don't care about me."

"Do you have family?"

"I have Claire."

"Your wife?"

"Not yet."

"Have you talked with her about this shooting?"

"No. You're the only person I've told. The first night you saw me was the night of the shooting. I only came in here to hide."

"But you came back," Father Walters said.

Darrell met his gaze. "Yes. I did."

"Perhaps God is calling you."

"Burke said I needed Jesus in my life," he admitted.

"Who's Burke?"

"Someone I work with."

"He's a very wise man."

Darrell noticed how light it was getting outside and stood up. "I have to leave."

Father Walters stood with him and together they left the room.

"Talk to your Claire and see what she thinks you should do," he counseled.

"I don't want her to know." Darrell believed she would be safer in ignorance.

"But this is serious—and she is involved."

Darrell realized he was right. Claire was caught up in this because of him.

"Think about it. I only want you to be safe."

"You're not the only one." Darrell tucked his

hands in his pockets and slipped out of the church.

The priest watched him leave. He offered up a prayer for the troubled young man.

Father Walters wasn't the only one praying. Darrell repeated the Our Father over and over again as he made his way home. He didn't feel safe until he was inside the building, out of sight of the street.

Mark lay in bed, staring at the ceiling. It was after seven. He knew he should get up and drive to the office, but he hadn't slept much through the night and had little energy this morning.

The problem wasn't business. The deal he was working on was coming along nicely. Basically, life was good. His mother was still away. He'd called Christine and would be going with her for the weekend. Yet, in spite of everything he had to be grateful for, the fact that he'd seen Jenny again was still haunting him.

Mark all but threw himself out of bed—the bed he and Jenny had shared on several occasions. Memories of the loving, passionate times they'd spent there together were emblazoned on his soul. No one had ever meant as much to him as Jenny, and no one ever would. To this day, he didn't understand why his mother had been so averse to his relationship with Jenny.

His mother—

Mark had to admit that he was glad she was away. Seeing Jenny again had jarred him deeply and forced him to face up to the truth of what was in his heart. He needed this time away from his mother's influence to sort out his feelings. He needed time to figure out what had gone wrong. He was a man. How could he have been so weak, just when Jenny had needed him to be strong?

Sadly, Mark realized it was too late now to reclaim the beauty they had shared.

Nothing would ever be the same again.

Jenny was gone from his life.

Seton Leasing was his life now.

And he was due at the office within the hour.

Jenny was nervous as she lay, rosary in hand, in the hospital bed in a curtained-off area of the Emergency Room. She'd been there for almost two hours, being checked over and undergoing tests, and with each passing minute she was getting more and more worried about the health of her baby.

Her baby—

Tears welled in her eyes as she rested a soothing hand on the mound of her stomach. This was her child—her son or daughter. The thought that the child might have been harmed during her fall had filled her with anxiety. The fierce emotions that ravaged her only served to emphasize the difficulty of the decision she ultimately had to make about her baby. Did she dare keep her child and try to raise it on her own, or should she give it up to be adopted by a mother and father who could offer it the security of a two-parent home?

Jenny loved her baby. She only wanted what

was best for her child. She drew a ragged breath and offered up another frantic, silent prayer that the baby was safe.

The sound of voices just beyond the curtain interrupted Jenny's fervent prayer, and she looked up as Peggy, the ER nurse who'd been taking care of her, appeared with a clipboard in hand.

"Is my baby all right?" Jenny asked quickly, trying to read the nurse's expression.

"Your baby is fine," Peggy reassured her with a warm smile.

"Thank heaven."

"And you are, too, but Dr. Murray wants you to get more rest."

Jenny couldn't help laughing. "I'd love to, but some nights it's just not easy."

The nurse laughed, too, remembering her own pregnancies. "I understand, but take it as easy as you can."

"I will. I don't ever want to have another accident like this one."

"You were very lucky."

"I was blessed."

"Yes, you were," Peggy agreed. "You'll be sore for a few days. You have some bumps and bruises, but nothing was broken, and your baby is healthy."

"Thank you." The relief in her tone was evident.

Peggy helped her fill out the necessary paperwork, then left her to get dressed.

Donna was still in the waiting room and she

hurried to Jenny's side when she was released.

"Is everything all right?"

"Yes. Thank heaven, the baby wasn't hurt."

"What about you?"

"I'm fine, too," Jenny answered, and was surprised to find that she meant it. Learning her baby was healthy had been the best news she could get.

"Good. You ready to go home? I already called work and told the boss you wouldn't be in today."

"Thanks, Donna."

"You've got sick days, so you might as well use them."

They were leaving the ER when Jenny saw a sign on the wall that said "Chapel" and an arrow pointing the way.

"Donna, do you mind if I stop in the chapel for a minute?"

"Not at all. I'll go get the car and come back for you. Say a prayer for me while you're in there," Donna said with a grin.

"I will."

Jenny made her way down the hall to the chapel. It was small and dimly lit. There was no one else in it, and Jenny was glad. She slid into a pew and awkwardly knelt down. A statue of Mary holding baby Jesus was on one side of the chapel, and Jenny felt a pang of deep emotion as she stared at the Blessed Mother and Child.

She offered up her thanks, then prayed, "Oh, God, please help me make the right decision. Please help me to know what I should do."

Jenny closed her eyes and bowed her head, listening for an answer. She'd always thought life would be so much easier if God would simply call or e-mail or fax the answers to her prayers, instead of leaving her to flounder around searching for His will.

Quiet reigned in the peaceful chapel.

After a few moments, Jenny knew she had to leave to meet Donna.

She opened her eyes again.

And it was then that she saw it.

There in the pew ahead of her was a pacifier.

She stared down at the pacifier in amazement, wondering why she hadn't noticed it before. With utmost care, she picked it up.

Her heart filled with joy.

She knew now what she should do.

She would keep her baby.

Jenny's smile broadened even more when she realized that God had answered her prayer, but He hadn't given away whether her baby was a boy or a girl. The pacifier was yellow. She tucked it in her pocket and left the chapel. She couldn't wait to tell Donna that she had made her decision.

CHAPTER EIGHT

Tina was smiling as she put on the last of her makeup.

Soon she would be at the office.

Soon she would see Alan again.

Her smile broadened as she studied her reflection. Her makeup was perfect, and so was her hair. She was ready to entice him.

She'd deliberately spent the night apart from Alan. She'd lied to him when she told him she wasn't feeling well, and had left him at his hotel to return home to her own apartment alone. She had to make sure he continued to want her. She didn't want to risk losing the mystique that kept him intrigued with her. Her relationship with Alan was all about power, and she was determined to use whatever means necessary to achieve her goal.

And her goal was to rise as quickly as she could through the ranks at Warson-Freeman.

Using rich, powerful men was the best way to achieve that end.

For a moment, Tina thought of her mother. She didn't dwell on her home life often, but her mother's miserable existence was the reason for her determination to succeed—by whatever means necessary.

Her mother had been trapped in a loveless life—Tina's father had deserted them when she was a baby. Her mother had gotten a divorce and had married a second time to a man she'd believed would love them and take care of them.

Her mother had been wrong.

Her stepfather had been a drunk, and physically abusive as well, but for some reason, her mother wouldn't leave him. She'd claimed to love him and had actually defended him to Tina when her daughter had urged her to get out while she could. Tina had worked two jobs to put herself through college, and she'd been away at school when her mother had died, a lonely, pathetic woman.

Tina had made up her mind that she would never find herself in the same situation as her mother. She would turn the tables on men. She would take what they offered, but she would use them for her own ends. She would take care of herself. She would never need a man or love one.

Love—

Tina scoffed at the idea of love. Romantic movies and romance novels were for dreamers. She knew the truth about life, and it wasn't pretty.

There were no heroes in real life—no knights in shining armor to show up and rescue you just when you needed them most. Money and power were what kept you safe, and that was what she wanted. That was what she was going to get—any way she could.

Ready for the excitement of the day to come, Tina left her apartment and headed for Warson-Freeman. The sky was the limit for her career.

Joe ordered his usual large, fully leaded coffee and a sausage-and-egg biscuit, then took his tray and started off to find an empty table. Gail was working this morning, so the day was his to do with as he pleased, and already he was frustrated. He'd been ready to talk to Jenny this morning, but she hadn't shown up at 6:30 Mass. He hoped nothing was wrong with her, and had even offered up a quick prayer at church for her safety. He couldn't help wondering if she'd gone into labor and was at the hospital. Her time was close, that was for sure. If she did go into labor and Father Beck heard, Joe hoped the priest would let him know. He wanted to help out in any way he could.

As Joe moved through the restaurant, he noticed Dorothy Pennington sitting by herself reading the morning paper, and he decided to see if she wanted company.

"Morning, Dorothy," Joe greeted her.

"Why, Joe." She smiled up at him. "Sit down. I saw you at church, but I didn't know you'd be coming here, too."

"I'm off today, but Gail's working this morning, so fast food sounded a lot better than my own cooking."

"I know what you mean. How have you been? How are your grandchildren?" she asked as he settled in opposite her.

They chatted easily, having known each other for years through church.

"What about you? What have you been up to?" Joe asked.

"I'm fine. I spoke with David and Carol last night. They're both doing fine, too," she told him, avoiding the ugliness in her life.

Dorothy told herself she wasn't lying to Joe. There just seemed no point in revealing the sordid details of her current existence. She hadn't even told Father Walters yet. It was too humiliating. She'd only told Paige because she'd hoped to get a job at the boutique.

"That's good to hear," Joe said. "You don't happen to know where Jenny Emerson was this morning, do you?"

"No. I don't speak with her that often. Why?"

"I wanted to talk to her and see if she needed any help, with the new baby coming and all."

"She must be excited."

"I'm sure she is."

They both remembered how their own anticipation had grown years before as their children's due dates neared.

"Life is good," Joe remarked with an easygoing grin.

Dorothy didn't say a word. She couldn't.

Joe didn't know why, but he suddenly sensed an uneasiness in Dorothy.

"Did I ever give you one of my rosaries?" he asked.

"No."

"Well, here." Joe dug deep in his pocket and pulled out a small plastic bag holding a hand-made, and already blessed, rosary. He held it out to her across the table.

"It's beautiful." Dorothy took the bag and opened it to take out the rosary. "You're very talented. May I pay you for it?"

"No," he refused. "I don't do it for money. I do it for God."

"You're a wonderful man, Joe Myers." She grinned at him.

"I know that, but you'd better tell Gail!" he chuckled.

They finished eating and walked out of the restaurant together.

"Have a wonderful day, Joe."

"You, too, Dorothy. You stay out of trouble," he teased.

"Do I have to?"

"On second thought—nah. Go have some fun."

They parted, and Dorothy found herself wondering if she just might have fun today. She checked her watch and found it was almost 9 A.M. She was surprised that time had passed so quickly, talking with Joe. Her children had advised her to see to her finances this morning, so her next stop was the bank. She would open a checking account in her own name.

Alan was restless. He paced his office, edgy and tired. He had lain awake for most of the night, his thoughts on Tina. He worried about her being ill and wondered how she was feeling. He'd called down to her office as soon as he'd come into work an hour ago, but she hadn't arrived yet and still hadn't returned his call.

Stopping before his window, Alan stared out at the panoramic skyline. The sun was shining brightly. It was a beautiful day, and life would have been perfect if Tina had been there with him.

"Alan?"

He turned quickly to see her coming through the door. He smiled for the first time that day.

"Tina—"

"Your secretary said you were in. I hope you don't mind the interruption," Tina said, sounding professional and businesslike as she entered his office.

"No. Not at all. Come in," he invited. "Thanks, Kelly. Hold my calls for a few minutes."

"Yes, sir," his secretary called back.

Tina closed the door.

They were alone.

Alan didn't say another word. He just crossed the room and grabbed her up in his arms. His mouth devoured hers in a hungry, desperate kiss.

Inwardly, Tina celebrated her triumph. It had worked! By staying away from him, she'd made him desire her even more! She returned his embrace with abandon.

"I missed you," Tina said softly when they finally ended the kiss.

"And I missed you," Alan growled, refusing to release her.

"It was a long night."

"Too long," he said, and he kissed her again.

Alan heard Kelly speaking with someone in the outer office. He started to put Tina from him just as the office door burst open.

"Wait! Let me tell him you're here—" Kelly was saying, trying to protect her boss.

Alan turned, startled to see his son and daughter come through the door.

"David? Carol? What are you doing here?" he demanded, quickly distancing himself from Tina.

Tina spun around and recognized the two immediately from the pictures on Alan's desk. David was a much younger version of his father, and she might have found him attractive except for the look on his face as he glared at her. The girl was pretty, too, but her expression was as threatening as her brother's.

David had seen how the couple had jumped apart when he'd come through the door, and rage filled him. He looked from the young woman to his father in pure disgust, then looked back at the woman. "Get out."

"Excuse me?" Tina returned haughtily. He had no right to speak to her that way.

"My brother said to get out," Carol repeated, going to stand at David's side. "And I suggest you do what he said before I rip all your perfectly streaked, bleached-blond hair out of your head!"

"Alan?" Tina glanced his way, not quite sure if his daughter was serious or not.

"Go on. I'll call you later."

Tina started from the room with as much dignity as she could muster in the face of such open hostility. She was furious with Alan for sending her off this way in front of his son and daughter.

Carol watched Tina's every move as she passed by.

"Slut," Carol muttered.

"Why, you—!" Tina turned on her.

"What?" Carol sneered at the other woman. She was so close to her own age that it made her physically ill to think of her with her father. "You don't like hearing the truth?"

"Carol! Stop it!" Alan ordered, moving to stand between them. "Tina, I'll handle this. Go on back to work."

Tina let herself out and closed the door behind her, glad to get away. She'd imagined coming face-to-face with Alan's wife one day, but she'd never thought she'd run into his son and daughter. It was going to be interesting to see how Alan handled them. Remembering the kiss he'd just given her, she didn't think there would be a problem. Alan wanted her. She was certain of it. She was just irritated that he wasn't man enough to face down his children with her by his side.

"Is everything all right?" Kelly asked Tina as she passed by her desk. Kelly cast a puzzled look at the closed office door.

"Everything is fine," Tina replied blithely, returning to her role as professional businesswoman.

Kelly shrugged off her curiosity and went back to work. She'd been Alan's secretary long enough to know he could handle anything that came his way.

Alan stared at his two grown children. He was furious and, though he hated to admit it, embarrassed that they'd walked in on him with Tina.

"What are you doing here?" he demanded, covering his embarrassment with bravado.

"We thought we'd come by and see our father at work," David challenged.

"If that's what you call work." Carol's tone was dripping with sarcasm.

David didn't wait for his father to respond. He went on, "We spoke with Mom last night. What the hell is going on?"

"Your mother and I have separated," Alan began.

"The version I heard sounded more like you'd dumped her for a younger woman—and judging from what we just saw, I'd say that version is the right one."

"The point is—"

Carol interrupted him heatedly, "The point is, don't you remember 'forsaking all others'? That was part of a serious vow you took, wasn't it?"

Alan wasn't about to let his children dictate to him.

"Don't lecture me, young lady. I've had about enough from the two of you already," he said in his most autocratic tone. When they'd been young that tone had been very effective in controlling them. He was shocked now when David and Carol both ignored him.

"No," David said coldly. "We've had enough of you—and your slut! I always thought you were someone to look up to, but I know now I was wrong."

"And you always told me a man should be honorable! That he should protect and defend his own!" Carol told her father. "Don't you remember when you threw Matt Hudson out of our house after I told you he'd cheated on me with another girl? And now—now look at you! What you're doing is worse than anything Matt ever did!"

"How dare you treat our mother this way?" David demanded, outraged.

"Don't you use that tone with me, young man." Alan took a step toward him.

David was ready. He didn't hesitate. His rage was so overpowering that he decked his father with one fierce blow.

Kelly heard the crash in the office and charged from her desk. She threw open the office door to find her boss laid out flat on the floor, his son standing over him.

"Mr. Pennington!" she gasped, truly shocked. "Should I call security?"

"There's no need. We were just leaving," David said tightly.

He took his sister's arm and directed her out of the office past the secretary. Neither of them bothered to look back.

"Are you all right?" Kelly went to Alan's side.

"I'm fine." Alan got to his feet, shrugging off her attempt to help him. He wiped blood from the corner of his mouth.

She waited for a moment, hoping he would explain what had happened, but he said nothing more. "Would you like some ice for that?"

"Yes."

She quickly wrapped some ice in a cloth for him at the small bar in his office. After giving it to him, she left him alone.

Alan went to stand at his office window. He pressed the cold compress to his mouth and jaw. Only a short time before, he'd been filled with excitement over seeing Tina. Now, he felt only anger.

How dare his children invade his office this way?

How dare they lecture him on morals?

Turning away from the view, he went to check his reflection in the mirror. He had several important meetings today, and he had to make a good appearance. Satisfied that none of his business associates would be able to tell he'd been struck, he straightened his tie and returned to his desk. He kept the ice on his jaw a little longer as he resumed his paperwork. He tried to keep his thoughts focused on work—as best he could.

* * *

"Dorothy! What a pleasant surprise," Paige exclaimed, welcoming her to the boutique late that morning. After their last conversation, she'd feared she wouldn't be seeing her friend for a while.

"I'm glad you think so," Dorothy replied, returning her smile.

"What can I do for you today?" Paige noticed that something seemed different about the other woman.

"It's what I can do for you," Dorothy answered confidently.

"I don't understand."

"Let me explain. After our last conversation, I did some serious thinking. You know how much I love this store, and I told you I needed to start a career. That's why I have this." Dorothy reached in her purse and drew out a cashier's check. She handed it to Paige. "I'd like to buy into your business. I'd like to become your partner in Total Elegance. What do you say?"

Paige took the check and stared down at the amount. She blinked in surprise. "But—"

Dorothy was a bit nervous. She hadn't dealt in the business world much, and she wasn't sure of the best way to handle these kinds of dealings. She'd thought the amount was sufficient, but if Paige needed more, she could arrange it now that she'd taken care of her bank account—and emptied out Alan's. "If that's not enough—"

"No!" Paige blurted out, looking up at her. She

felt as if a great burden had been lifted off her soul. She couldn't imagine a better partner than Dorothy, and with this kind of backing, Total Elegance could advertise and even grow! "Oh, I'm interested in your offer, all right! Very interested!"

It was the answer Dorothy had been waiting to hear. Relief surged through her.

"Welcome to 'our' store, partner," Paige stuck out her hand to seal the deal.

"There is one other thing." Dorothy kept her expression serious, as she hesitated to take the younger woman's hand.

"What is it?" Paige was suddenly cautious.

"I want a discount on my clothes from now on." Dorothy broke into an impish grin.

Paige laughed out loud. "I think we can arrange that."

"Then it's a deal?"

"It's a deal."

They shook hands—a business handshake.

Then they hugged.

Paige's desperate prayers had been answered, and Dorothy felt a sense of hope for the first time in days.

CHAPTER NINE

"What do you mean you haven't found him?" the boss demanded, surging out of his desk chair in a rage.

"I've been there watching every morning, but there's been no sign of him."

The boss couldn't believe his underling's stupidity. His voice was steely as he ordered, "I told you to find him and I meant it. The man's not about to go back to the scene. He knows you saw him!"

"But—"

"Have you checked out any businesses in the area to see who works around there?"

"No."

"Do it!"

"But, boss, if he hasn't gone to the cops yet, he isn't going to."

The boss turned his most threatening glare on

him. "I don't want any loose ends. Find the son of a bitch and make sure he never gets the chance to talk. Do you understand me?"

The man knew better than to argue. He hurried from the room.

Joanne knocked on Mark's office door and opened it when he called for her to come in.

"I'm leaving now," she told him. "Do you need anything else before I go?"

"I'm just fine," Mark told her with an easy smile. "It has been a very good day."

"Yes, it has," she agreed, knowing he'd closed the deal he'd been working on that very afternoon. "Congratulations."

"Thanks."

"I was praying on it for you," Joanne told him with a grin.

"You were?" Mark was honestly surprised.

"Absolutely. Nothing works better."

"So, you're well connected, are you? How about praying for winning lottery numbers? Then we could all retire."

"I don't think God concerns Himself too much with lotteries," she laughed. "Besides, why would you want to retire? You're good at what you do."

"It's just a dream, I guess—sitting on a beach somewhere, taking it easy."

"You'd be bored out of your mind in no time."

"You know me too well." Mark laughed with her.

"That's what secretaries are for. Now, back to business. Tomorrow you're leaving early, right?"

"Yes, I'm spending the weekend at the Barretts' lodge."

"Good, you deserve to have some fun after this week. Do you have a number there?"

"No, just call my cell phone if you need to reach me. Is there anything pressing I should take care of in the morning?"

"The usual. Your mother's not due back in town until Saturday, so there's nothing too exciting."

"I'll see you tomorrow, then. Have a good night."

"You, too."

Joanne left him, and Mark turned back to finishing the last of the paperwork before leaving for the gym. He was most satisfied with the way everything had turned out. Some days definitely were better than others.

Darrell had passed a tough day. He'd gotten little sleep, tossing and turning, worrying about what the priest had advised him to do.

The priest was right.

Claire was in danger now.

And it was all because of him!

Darrell had never cared this much about anyone before. He loved Claire. She meant everything to him. He couldn't allow her to be put at risk. He had to find a way to keep her safe.

Fury ate at him. Why had he been fated to be in that one place on that particular day? Why?

The counseling he'd received had worked. He knew he was responsible for his own actions. He knew if anything happened to Claire, he would be to blame for not confiding in her.

So Darrell accepted what he had to do. And he waited tensely for her to come home from work.

It was only a short time later that Claire returned, but to Darrell it seemed as if hours had passed. He welcomed her with a kiss, and she eagerly returned his embrace. He held her close for a moment, treasuring the joy of having her in his arms before letting her go.

"I do like coming home to you," she told him with a grin. "I just wish you didn't have to leave for work so soon."

"So do I," he agreed solemnly.

She heard his dark tone and frowned, wondering at it. "Is something wrong?" she asked, looking up at him. "You look tired tonight. Didn't you get any sleep?"

"Not much."

"How come? Were the neighbors noisy?"

"No. Nothing like that. I was thinking, that's all."

"About what?"

"I need to talk to you, Claire," Darrell told her, releasing her and stepping away.

He seemed so intent, so troubled, that she feared what was coming. "What is it?" She was holding her breath, afraid he was about to tell her he was leaving her.

"Sit down."

An iciness grew within Claire.

She'd thought things were going well for them. They were both working and paying their bills.

She'd thought things were okay.

And now—

"Why? What's happened?"

"It's bad."

She waited.

"The other morning after I got off work, I saw something I wasn't supposed to see."

Claire frowned, confused. "I don't understand."

Darrell told her everything, from the shooting to talking with the priest.

"You told a priest?" She was shocked.

"I had to tell someone. I didn't know what to do. They won't give up until they find me."

"That's why you changed coats and hats the other day." Claire understood now.

"I had to disguise myself. I'm taking a different way to work every night. I'm making myself scarce on the streets, but when the priest told me you were in danger just by being around me, I had to tell you."

"Oh, Darrell—"

Claire went to him and wrapped her arms around him. She held him tight, needing to reassure him, and herself.

Darrell returned her embrace. He lost himself in the sweet beauty of her love. He loved her more than he'd ever loved anyone in his life. But he was afraid. So afraid.

"So this is why you were talking about getting away from here the other day," she remarked, remembering their conversation.

"Believe me, baby, if I could I'd pack us up and

leave right now, but that would only make things worse. Everybody would be looking for me then."

"And you wouldn't have been guilty of anything except trying to stay alive," Claire said, her fear turning to outrage. "There's only one thing you can do."

"Crawl in a hole and never come out?"

"No. You have to tell the police what you know."

"They aren't going to listen to me!"

"Yes, they will," she insisted. "I'll go with you to the station if you want."

"It won't do any good," he persisted. "Nobody will believe me. I'm an ex-con."

"Darrell—someone was murdered! You can identify who did it. You need to do this. You served your time, and you're living a clean life now. The police will appreciate your help."

"But if I go to the cops and they make an arrest, the killers will come gunning for me."

"Not if they're locked up."

"There has to be more than just the gunman."

"Then we have to help the cops get all of them."

When he didn't respond, Claire knew he was weighing his choices. She waited a minute to give him time to think things through.

"Darrell, if what you believe is true, they're already looking for you. You have no choice. We have to go to the police. It's the right thing to do."

He looked up at her, his expression almost tortured. "The right thing, huh? I haven't done the right thing very often in my life."

"Then it's time to start," she encouraged him.

"I'm due to see Schmidt tomorrow. I'll ask him what to do. He'll know how to handle it."

"I know what kind of man you are, Darrell." Claire hugged him close again. "You're a brave man. You wouldn't have told the priest if you hadn't cared, and you wouldn't have told me, either."

Darrell had never considered himself the least bit brave. He'd always thought he was only doing what he had to do to survive. Even now, his instincts were still telling him to find a good place to hide and wait it out.

His heart, however, was urging him to act.

He didn't know where he'd find the strength, but he would do it.

He would be the man Claire believed him to be.

Darrell was praying that he'd made the right decision as he went off to work later that night.

Tina was ready and waiting for Alan when he arrived at her apartment that night. They had managed only one short phone conversation since she'd left him that morning in his office, and she was intensely curious about what had gone on with his son and daughter. She had dinner ready and waiting for him, and had donned a tight shirt, shorts and strappy sandals just to entice him. She knew how much he loved her legs, and she used that knowledge to her advantage whenever she could.

"You're here—at last," she greeted him, not bothering to wait for his knock. She had watched him from the parking lot and opened the door just as he reached the hallway.

"Not a minute too soon," Alan growled.

He stepped into her apartment and kicked the door shut behind him. Tina was in his arms immediately, kissing him hungrily. She drew back when he made a small strange sound.

"Is something wrong?" she asked, and then she noticed his swollen bottom lip. She was shocked. "Oh—I'm sorry. What happened to you?"

Alan ducked his head, embarrassed at his show of weakness. "It doesn't matter. Come back here."

He drew her close again and tried to kiss her, but she eluded him.

"Not until you tell me what happened, Alan," Tina insisted, reaching up to touch his face. Suddenly she realized what must have happened. "Did your son hit you?"

"It's nothing." He didn't want to talk about his argument with David and Carol.

"I wondered how your visit with your children went. Now I guess I know." She sounded sympathetic. "Would you like some ice to put on it?"

"No. Right now all I want is you."

Tina purred, feeling powerful and in control. "I like the way you think."

She took his hand and led him to the bedroom. Dinner could wait.

Jenny had passed a quiet day since returning from the ER, and she was curled up in bed now, eating ice cream and reading intently from the book she held. Beside her on the bed was a notepad and pen, and every now and then she stopped to make a note.

"Hmmmm, Ellen Emerson," she said to herself as she wrote out the name and studied it. "No, too many Es. Let's see—"

Jenny paged through the baby name book slowly, studying the names. She wanted to pick a girl's name and a boy's name, so she would be ready when the baby came. Family names came to mind. There were Patricias and Cassandras and Georges and Jims in the family tree, but none of them stood out.

When she came to the "Ms" in the girls' section, she spotted the name Margo and immediately turned to the boy's section. She certainly wouldn't name her baby after Mark's mother. There were a lot of boys' names she liked—Adam and Brett and Rick and Steve. She paused at Mark, scoffing as she read the meaning: "warlike one." There was nothing warlike about a man who let his mother dictate to him.

If her baby was a boy, Jenny was not going to name him after his biological father.

Jenny jotted down Steve Emerson and Rick Emerson on her notepad and smiled. She liked them both. Then she looked through the girls' names again.

Finishing her ice cream, she put aside the book, paper and pen and turned out the light. Tomorrow was a workday. She needed to rest, for over the weekend she planned to start redecorating the extra bedroom and turn it into a nursery. Jenny knew she had a lot to do before young Steve or Rick or Nicole or Jackie arrived.

Her heart swelled with love at the thought of her child.

Soon . . . very soon . . .

CHAPTER TEN
DAY FOUR

Guide me, Lord. . .

Darrell entered the church. He quietly slid into an empty pew and dropped to his knees on the kneeler. His mother had always made fun of Catholics for kneeling to pray, but Darrell understood it. He felt humbled before the Lord.

Mass hadn't started yet, so Darrell took advantage of the quiet time to offer up some fervent prayers. So much was happening in his life, he needed all the help he could get.

Darrell heard the door open behind him, and he tensed. He glanced cautiously back to see who'd come in, fearing he'd been spotted and followed inside. He was glad to see it was only the pregnant woman coming down the main aisle. She smiled at him as she settled in the pew across from him, and he found himself smiling back.

Darrell was hoping to see Father Walters today, but it was the younger priest who entered to say the Mass. Darrell forced his disappointment aside and tried to concentrate on the Gospel.

The Mass seemed to pass quickly this morning.

"Let us offer each other the sign of peace," Father Beck intoned.

Darrell was surprised when the young woman crossed the aisle and offered him her hand.

"Peace be with you," she said, shaking his hand.

"You, too," he answered, unsure exactly what to do. No one had ever approached him before in this way.

She met his gaze forthrightly, and it almost seemed she could look into the depths of his very soul. The intensity of her regard startled him, but then she was gone, slipping back into her own pew and turning her attention back to the altar.

When it was time for Communion, Darrell left by the side door. He hoped to run into Father Walters, but there was no sign of him anywhere.

Anxious to get home to Claire, he didn't linger. She had taken the day off work to go with him to see Schmidt. He was glad. He needed all the moral support he could get.

"Jenny—wait up a minute," Joe called out as they left Our Lady after Mass.

Jenny had already started down the steps, but she stopped at his call and turned back. "Good morning, Mr. Myers."

"Yes, it is," he agreed, coming to stand with her, "but I think it's time you started calling me Joe."

"Joe?"

"That's right. 'Mr. Myers' makes me feel real old, and I'm not ready to admit to that yet, no matter how true it may be," he chuckled.

Jenny laughed, too.

"How are you doing?" Joe asked.

"I'm fine."

"Gail and I would love to have you over for dinner one night, if you've got the time?"

She was surprised by the invitation, even though her parents had been friends with Mr. and Mrs. Myers. "I haven't seen Mrs. . . . . Gail in what seems like forever."

"She was saying the same thing about you just the other night. You want to come?"

"Sure. That would be nice. When do you want me?"

"You busy tonight? We'll probably eat around six."

"Tonight sounds great. I'll be there."

"Good. We'll see you then."

"How did your week go?" Stan Schmidt asked Darrell once he'd settled in the chair across the desk from him. He'd been watching Darrell closely ever since he'd come into his office. There was something different about him today. His body language and the shiftiness of his eye contact told Stan something wasn't quite right. He intended to find out what was going on.

"Here's my paycheck stub." Darrell handed it over for him to inspect.

"Good." Stan checked it and handed it back. "Looks like you're staying out of trouble."

"I've been trying to. You aren't going to test me for drugs this time?"

"Are you clean?"

"Yeah."

"I'll trust you on that." Stan fixed him with a penetrating look. "You seem to have everything under control, so what's troubling you?"

Darrell wasn't surprised that Stan had picked up on his nervousness. Stan had a reputation as a fine parole officer, and he'd just proven it. Darrell looked up at him and made direct eye contact for the first time.

"Something happened," he admitted.

"What happened, Darrell?"

He hesitated.

"I'm here to help you," Stan encouraged.

"I don't know if you can. I don't know if anybody can."

"Why?"

Darrell paused for a moment to gather his courage before going on. "A couple of days ago, I saw something I wasn't supposed to see."

"What?"

"Did you hear about that shooting the other morning?"

"I read about it, yes."

"I was on my way home from work, and I witnessed the whole thing."

Stan was shocked. "You know who did it?"

"I'd recognize him if I ever saw him again."

"You should have gone to the police right away," Stan advised, even though he completely understood why Darrell had remained silent.

Darrell had known Stan was going to say that, but the remark still irritated him. "I was scared. Hell, I still am."

"The gunman saw you?"

He nodded. "That's why I've been trying to stay out of sight ever since."

Stan knew Darrell's position was serious. "You need to talk to the police."

"I know, but I wanted to tell you first."

"Let me make a phone call."

Darrell fell silent, listening as Stan called the police station and requested that an officer be sent to his office.

After hanging up, Stan gave him a tight smile. "Someone will be here shortly. Then we'll see what we can do about your situation. Hopefully, they'll be able to make a quick arrest with the information you provide."

"I hope so."

"So do I." Stan understood all too well what could happen if things didn't go right.

"Yes, this is Alan Pennington," Alan said into the phone in his office.

"Mr. Pennington, this is Henry McMillan at First State Bank. There seems to be some problem with your accounts."

Alan frowned, puzzled by the tone of the man's voice. "I don't understand."

"Mr. Pennington, your accounts are overdrawn. I've covered several checks for you, but I thought it was important to alert you to the situation. You need to make sure that the problem is rectified as quickly as possible."

"This must be the bank's error. There's plenty of money in my accounts!" Alan started to argue with him, but a sudden sinking feeling took hold of him. *Dorothy!* He had never thought Dorothy would go behind his back to take money out of their joint accounts. He'd thought the lawyers would work out an amicable settlement. He should have realized—

"Sir?" McMillan's tone turned cold. "I think it would be best if you came in to the bank so we can meet to discuss this."

"I'll be there shortly."

Alan hung up the phone, angry and embarrassed. He immediately called home, but Dorothy didn't answer. Disgusted, he stormed out of the office.

"You're going out?" Kelly asked in surprise as he strode past her desk. She saw his hostile expression and wondered what had happened.

"Yes. I have an unexpected meeting I have to attend. Did my paycheck come down yet?"

"Yes. I have it right here." She handed him his pay envelope. "What should I tell anyone who calls?"

"Tell them I'm out of the office, but I should be back shortly."

Kelly watched him as he walked out. He seemed like a man on a mission. She was glad she wasn't standing in his way.

"Is there anything else you remember from that morning that might help us make an arrest?" Officer Anderson asked, continuing to take notes. He was thankful for the break in the case and anxious to get as many details as he could from Darrell Miller. It had been several days since the murder, and until Parole Officer Schmidt's phone call, they had been no closer to solving the crime than on the first day.

"I was a block away, and it was still half dark," Darrell explained. "But like I said, the car was a late model black Chevy and the license plate had the numbers 219 on it."

"Are you sure about the numbers?"

"I'm positive. February 19—2/19—is my girlfriend's birthday."

"What about the driver? You say you'd recognize him if you saw him again?"

"That's right."

"How can you be so sure you can identify the suspect, when he was that far away?"

"That man was ugly. I'll never forget his face."

"He was a white man with dark hair and a big nose, right?"

"Yes."

"All right, Mr. Miller, I want you to keep a low profile and contact us immediately if you see the car or this man again. Do you understand?"

"I understand, all right."

"We'll have an officer keeping an eye on things for you."

"Good," Stan put in. "Mr. Miller is cooperating fully, and he deserves all the protection we can give him."

"We'll do what we can," Officer Anderson assured the parole officer.

"Can I leave? Get out of town?" Darrell asked.

"No, I'm sorry," Stan told him.

The police officer stood and shook hands with Stan, then turned to Darrell and offered him his hand, too. "Thank you for your help."

Darrell was surprised by the gesture, but he stood up and shook his hand. "Get them."

"We will," Officer Anderson answered with confidence.

When he'd gone, closing the office door behind him, Stan looked at Darrell.

"You did the right thing," he told him.

"I hope so."

"I'm sure they'll have somebody driving past your place and checking things out for you. You just make sure to keep a low profile, like he said."

"I will."

"If you need me, Darrell, call me at any time. Otherwise, I'll see you next month."

Darrell left the office to find Claire waiting patiently for him in the lobby. She looked up and smiled when she saw him coming. Just the sight of her eased any doubts Darrell had about what he'd done.

He had revealed what he knew to the cops to keep her safe.

Claire was all that mattered.

"How did it go?" Claire asked.

He shrugged. "I told them what I knew. Now let's hope they find him."

"I'm proud of you," she said earnestly, gazing up at him with pure love and respect.

Darrell had never heard anyone praise him that way before. "You are?"

"Yes. You're a good man, Darrell. I love you." She spoke softly so no one else could hear, only Darrell.

"Let's get out of here and go home."

He looked around cautiously as they left the building.

He could never let his guard down.

There was too much at risk.

Alan hung up the phone in thorough disgust. It had been as bad as he'd feared at the bank, and now he'd just learned that Dorothy's lawyer had already spoken with his attorney. Since Alan was responsible for the breakup of the marriage, he was going to pay. He made a handsome salary at Warson-Freeman. Dorothy's lawyer knew it and he was going after Alan for every penny he could get—and then some. The divorce was going to hurt.

A knock sounded at his office door.

"Yes?" he called out tersely, annoyed by the interruption.

Kelly opened the door and stuck her head in to tell him, "Miss Lawrence is here to see you. She says she has an appointment with you."

Kelly sounded doubtful, for there was nothing marked on her calendar. She kept careful track of his schedule so he never missed an important meeting.

"Yes." Alan was jarred from his disturbing thoughts of the divorce. He and Tina didn't have an appointment, but he always encouraged her to slip away from her work and come to him any time she got the chance. "Thank you, Kelly. Show her in."

A moment later Tina came into the room and closed the door behind her. Alan didn't say a word. He just stood up and went to her.

Tina saw his troubled expression and went straight into his arms.

"Is something wrong?" she asked sweetly, drawing him down for a passionate kiss.

He savored her closeness, enjoying the heated, forbidden exchange.

"It's nothing," Alan told her when they finally moved apart.

"Are you sure? You look worried."

"It's just business." He did not want to discuss his suddenly difficult financial situation.

"In that case, what can we do tonight to make you forget about business and smile again? I should be finished here by six. Do you want to go out to dinner or eat in?"

"In sounds good," he answered, his gaze devouring her. He was hungry, all right, but for her, not food. He would have taken her right then and there, but after the encounter with David and Carol, he knew the danger of giving in to his desire for her at the office.

"I'll see you at my place. How's seven sound?"

"I'll be there."

Tina left him. She was looking forward to the evening to come.

Alone again, Alan returned to sit at his desk. His mood had not improved. The reality of what his life had become stayed with him. No matter what he did, there was no hiding from it.

Officer Anderson reported back to his sergeant, filling him in on everything he'd learned in his meeting with Stan Schmidt and Darrell Miller.

"Very good," Sergeant Williams said with a grim, determined smile. "The partial on the license plate is a big help. I'll start running a check on this right away."

"Are we going to have someone keeping track of Miller?"

"Yes. I want someone watching his house. The shooter knows there was a witness. He's not going to give up until he finds him. There have been too many shootings in that neighborhood. I want them stopped."

"We'll do all we can."

"This is our best chance yet to put an end to the violence."

"Let's do it."

Officer Anderson and Sergeant Williams shared a serious look. Anderson understood his sergeant's fierce conviction. The man who'd been gunned down the week before had been an honest, hard-working storekeeper on his way to open his small convenience shop. The police had found no connection to drug rings or gangs in his past. It seemed he had just been in the wrong place at the wrong time—just like Darrell Miller.

At least Miller was still alive.

Anderson wanted to make sure he stayed that way.

CHAPTER ELEVEN

Margo Seton went straight to the office from the airport. She'd caught an earlier flight than expected and was glad to be back in time to get some extra work done. It was late afternoon, and traffic was terrible as always on Friday. It never occurred to Margo to go home and relax, though. She wanted to catch up with Mark.

Margo had stayed in contact with Mark via e-mail, but they had not spoken for several days. She wanted to find out what had happened in the home office while she was away. Pulling into the parking lot at Seton Leasing's main office, she was surprised and a bit irritated to find that Mark's parking spot was empty. Hurrying inside, she went straight to his office to speak with Joanne.

"Mrs. Seton, welcome back," Joanne greeted her as she came to stand before her desk.

Margo was not in the mood for pleasantries or chit-chat. "Hello, Joanne. Where is Mark? I need to speak with him."

"He's gone for the day."

"Already?" Margo made a point of looking at her watch.

"Yes, ma'am. He told me to tell you he's going to be away all weekend."

"Where did he go?"

"He's spending the weekend with the Barrett family at their country estate."

"The Barretts?" Margo repeated. Her hostility immediately mellowed and a slow smile spread across her face.

"Yes, ma'am. You can try him on his cell phone, if you like, but he wasn't certain there would be service as far out in the woods as the place is. We didn't have the number for their lodge when he left, but I can try to reach him for you, if you'd like."

"No—no, that's all right. It's nothing urgent."

Margo was a bit disappointed Mark wasn't there. She had been anxious to talk business with him right away, but a liaison with the Barretts was more important. They were a powerful, well-connected family. Christine would make the perfect daughter-in-law. She was beautiful, smart and rich. It didn't get any better than that.

Margo's smile was satisfied as she made her way to her office. Mark was turning into the man she'd hoped he would be—a man driven to achieve—a man focused on what was really important. And that was Seton Leasing.

"I'm glad you could join us this weekend, Mark," Laura Barrett told Mark as they gathered in the main room of the spacious lodge.

It was near sunset, and they had all just unpacked and were ready to settle in and relax.

"I've been looking forward to it," Mark responded, impressed as he looked around. A massive stone fireplace dominated one wall, and a picture window on the opposite wall provided a panoramic view of a lake and the wooded hills beyond. "You have a beautiful place here."

"The land's been in the family for years. We only built the lodge five years ago. It's just far enough away from the city to be the perfect place to escape," Anthony Barrett said.

"How many acres do you own?"

"Close to three hundred," he answered, leading the way out onto the deck.

"Do you manage to come here often?"

"Anthony and I try to come up at least twice a month," Laura said, "but it's harder for Christine to find the time, as busy as her work schedule is. This weekend will be special, having you here."

"Yes, it will be," Christine agreed. Then looking at Mark, she invited, "Would you like to walk down to the lake?"

"Sounds good," Mark said.

"We'll be back," she told her parents.

Mark followed Christine from the deck and they started down the path to the boat dock.

Christine was eager to spend some time with Mark away from her parents' watchful eyes. It wasn't going to be easy to have many private moments this weekend, but she intended to do her best to be alone with him as often as she could.

"Do you like boating?" she asked.

"To tell you the truth, I've never done much of it."

"Well, we've got a party barge we can take out on the lake tomorrow. Or, if you want to move fast," she teased, giving him a suggestive look, "we've also got two jet skis."

"The jet skis sound like fun."

"I figured you'd like them, judging by your car," Christine laughed.

"It's fast, but it's definitely not made for country roads," Mark remarked, thinking of the bumpy ride after they'd left the interstate.

"You handled it well."

"Well, thanks."

"But tomorrow we'll find out just how well you can handle a jet ski."

"Is that a challenge?"

"I'd hate to beat you, since you are my guest," she said with a grin.

"I never back down from a dare."

"That's what I thought. I'll be looking forward to it."

"What does the winner win?" he asked. "What prize are we going for?"

"We can figure that out tomorrow."

"You're on, Christine."

Jenny had wondered all day what had possessed her to tell Joe Myers she'd join him and Gail for dinner tonight. True, they'd been friends of her parents, but she hadn't been close with them for years and she felt funny about socializing with them. But all her uncertainty evaporated the minute Gail opened the door and swept her into her arms.

"Jenny! Joe told me you were coming. I am so glad to see you! Come on in," Gail invited, giving her a quick hug and then stepping aside to let her pass.

"Thanks for having me over, Gail," Jenny said as she went into their small but cozy living room.

Gail took her coat and hung it in the hall closet.

"Excuse the mess," Gail said, gesturing toward the toy chest overflowing with toys in the far corner of the room. "The kids were here for a visit earlier, and I'm still cleaning up."

"How many grandchildren do you have now?"

"Two. A boy and a girl, and they're perfect, of course," she bragged.

"Of course," Jenny agreed with a smile. "Just like my baby is going to be." She knew there was no point in avoiding the topic. There was no doubt about her condition.

"Do you know what you're having yet?"

"No. I told the doctor I didn't want to know."

"I agree with you. It's more fun to be surprised." Gail led her toward the back of the house. "Let's go out to the kitchen. Dinner is just about ready. I hope you're hungry."

The kitchen was a spacious room, decorated with country crafts and family pictures. The door to the basement steps opened just as Jenny sat down at the table.

"I thought I heard the doorbell," Joe said with a smile as he spotted Jenny. "I'm glad you're here."

"Me, too."

"I'll start dishing up," Gail said.

Joe joined Jenny at the table while Gail brought out the food. When at last she sat down with them, Joe said grace.

Jenny was a bit surprised, but quickly joined in. She wondered how long it had been since she'd said a prayer over a meal.

"Amen," they all said at the same time.

"Or, as the grandkids say, 'Rub-a-dub-dub, thanks for the grub. Yeah, God!'" Joe added with a chuckle.

"I like that one."

"So do the kids."

Despite her initial uncertainty, Jenny found herself completely at ease with Gail and Joe as they enjoyed their dinner. Gail was a wonderful cook. The couple reminisced with Jenny about times they'd spent with her parents when she was younger.

"I still miss them a lot," Jenny admitted.

"You always will," Gail told her. "And especially with the baby coming. Do you have someone around to help you? Is the baby's father with you?"

"No. I'm going to do this on my own."

Gail gave her a reassuring smile. "You are a very strong woman, Jenny. It was hard for me, and I had Joe to help out. I can't imagine raising a baby alone."

"And I can't imagine not doing it," she told them. "It wasn't easy to decide. I wanted to make sure I was doing the best thing for my baby, and I'm certain now that I am." She told them about her visit to the church-sponsored center.

"It's good that you went for counseling," Joe said.

"What about the baby's father? Is it Mark? That young man you were seeing last summer?" Gail asked in a gentle tone.

"Yes. Mark's the father."

"He is going to help you, isn't he?"

"As far as I know, he doesn't even realize I'm still pregnant," Jenny answered tightly.

"So you did tell him?" Joe said, puzzled.

"Oh, yes. I told him, but we didn't see eye-to-eye about this pregnancy, so I broke off our relationship."

Joe and Gail instantly knew what she wasn't saying. Obviously, Mark had refused to take any responsibility for the pregnancy.

"I'm so sorry," Gail sympathized.

"I'm not."

Jenny's tone was such that Gail didn't ask more.

"When's your due date?"

"Any time now," she answered. "It's really kind of scary, to think it's so close."

"Do you have everything you need?"

"To tell you the truth, I just made the final decision to keep the baby yesterday. So I haven't had much time to think about it." She quickly told them about her fall, going to the hospital and finding the pacifier in the chapel.

"Thank God you weren't seriously injured," Joe said. "I wondered where you were at church yesterday. I missed seeing you."

"Believe me, I would rather have been at church with you than lying in the ER, worrying about losing my baby."

"The good news is that you and the baby are fine," Gail said.

"That's right."

"Have you picked out any names yet?"

Jenny grinned. "I was working on that last night, going through a baby name book."

"And?"

"Well, if it's a boy, I like Steve or Rick. If it's a girl, Nicole or Jackie. What do you think?"

"I like them all."

"So do I. I wonder how I'll finally decide."

"Once you're holding your baby in your arms, you'll know which name is right," Gail advised.

"You made the right decision," Joe praised her.

"Thanks." Jenny's gaze met Joe's and she saw pure love there. It warmed her soul.

"I've still got a lot to do. I had a rough few days with my car being in the shop, but it's fixed now and I've got the whole weekend ahead of me. I'm going to spend it turning my extra bedroom into a nursery." She was excited about the project.

"If you want help, just let us know," Joe said.

"I should be all right," she responded, not wanting to impose on anyone. "I've got the bassinet my mother used when I was little and an extra chest of drawers."

They chatted for another hour before Jenny got ready to go home.

Gail and Joe each gave her a warm hug. They stood together in the doorway of their home, watching Jenny drive away. They went in only after she'd disappeared from sight.

"I think Jenny needs a surprise shower tomorrow. What do you think?" Gail was already planning how to pull it off on such short notice.

"I think you're a wonderful woman," Joe said as he slipped an arm around her waist and gave her a quick hug. "No wonder I married you."

"You didn't marry me for my money?" she teased. She remembered the early years of their marriage when times had been hard and money tight. They'd had to scrimp and save just to make ends meet.

"No, I married you for your looks," he countered.

"You are such a charmer, Joe Myers!"

Gail gave him a quick kiss. As they moved apart, her expression faltered.

"I just wish Mark had done the right thing and married Jenny when they found out she was with child."

"That doesn't matter now," Joe said.

"You're right. What matters is that Jenny is doing the right thing, so we have to help her all we can. We have to give her that shower!"

"Who do you want me to call?" he volunteered, knowing that once his wife got an idea into her head, there was no stopping her.

"Well, we can start with Eileen and Audrey. I know they'll pitch in. Then you can call Ginny and Roberta, and ask them to call Judy, Karen, Rita and Jean, too."

"We can't forget Mary!"

"You're right. I'll call her as soon as I've talked to Eileen and Audrey. Once we get our little phone chain started, there will be no stopping us!"

"What do you say I fix up our crib and give that to her?"

"You're right, a bassinet isn't going to last long. She'll need a real crib."

"I'll get started on it right now."

"This is going to be so much fun!" Gail was already planning what cake to bake and what refreshments to get.

They would surprise Jenny at her home the following day and pitch in to help her with the redecorating.

It was going to be a wonderful time!

CHAPTER TWELVE
DAY FIVE

Lord, Give Me Strength. . .

Alan came awake and lay unmoving in Tina's bed. His head was pounding, and the sunlight streaming into the room only made the pain worse. He silently berated himself for having too much to drink the night before. At the time, though, he'd needed to lose himself in liquor—and in Tina's arms.

Tina—

She slumbered on beside him, unaware of his inner turmoil, and he was glad. They had passed a long, hot, passionate night together, but this morning, sex was the last thing on his mind.

It was a new day.

He had to face the harsh reality of what his life had become.

Money—

Yes, money was a problem now. His visit with the banker the day before had shown him just how dire his financial situation was. Dorothy had emptied their joint accounts. He was broke except for his paycheck. He'd opened a new account in his name only and had covered the bounced checks before permanently closing the joint accounts. His conversation with his attorney late yesterday afternoon had only emphasized how serious his position was right now. He had only a few viable options.

With money so tight, the plans he had discussed with Tina about finding an apartment for him this weekend would have to be put on hold. He couldn't even think about that until he got everything back under control. He didn't know where he was going to live until then, though, for living at the hotel was even more expensive on a day-to-day basis than taking an apartment. The trouble was, apartment managers always wanted a deposit, and high and dry as Alan was, he couldn't provide one. Nor did he want to tell Tina about his predicament.

"Good morning," Tina purred, coming to life beside him. She stretched sinuously and raised herself up on her elbow to gaze down at him. She kept the sheet covering her breasts, but let it fall low enough to entice.

Alan looked up at her. She looked beautiful. He was surprised that he felt no immediate surge of desire. If anything, all he felt was old and tired. "Good morning," he responded, his voice a low, husky growl.

Tina leaned toward him and kissed him. He

NAME: _____

ADDRESS: _____

_____

_____

TELEPHONE: _____

E-MAIL: _____

_____ I want to pay by credit card.

__ Visa   __ MasterCard   __ Discover

Account Number: _____

Expiration date: _____

SIGNATURE: _____

*Send this form, along with $2.00 shipping
and handling for your FREE books, to:*

Historical Romance Book Club
20 Academy Street
Norwalk, CT 06850-4032

*Or fax (must include credit card
information!) to:* 610.995.9274.
*You can also sign up on the Web
at* www.dorchesterpub.com.

Offer open to residents of the U.S. and
Canada only. Canadian residents, please
call 1.800.481.9191 for pricing information.

didn't respond in his usual hot-blooded manner, and she was a bit surprised. "Are you feeling all right?"

"Why?"

"You don't seem your usual self."

"Maybe it's because you wore me out last night."

"You think so?"

"I know so." He gave her another quick kiss and sat up to get out of bed.

"Would you like some breakfast?" Tina asked. "I've got eggs and bacon."

"That'll be great."

Tina got up, too. They both dressed and headed for the kitchen.

Alan was glad she'd been so easily distracted from wanting to make love. He had too many serious issues on his mind to want to indulge in lovemaking.

Alan set their place settings and sat down while Tina did the cooking.

"I went through yesterday's paper and marked a few places I thought you might like." She pointed to the real estate section she'd left on the table.

He picked up the pages to read the ones she'd circled.

Three-bedroom townhouse, close to everything. Newer carpet, two-car garage. FSBO. $140,000.

Two-bedroom apartment. Complex has pool, tennis courts and workout spa. $1200/month. Deposit required.

One-bedroom apartment. $650/month.

Silently Alan cursed his situation. The way things stood, he didn't even have the money to rent the one-bedroom apartment, for he was still legally responsible for all the expenses at his and Dorothy's home.

"What do you think?" Tina asked as she set a plate of bacon, eggs and toast before him. "Do you want to look at any of them today? If the one you decide on is vacant, you could move in as soon as you sign the contract."

"I'm going to have to wait until I speak with my attorney. I put a call in to him Friday, but he had already left the office for the weekend."

"Why? Is your wife giving you trouble?" Tina asked astutely as she joined him at the table.

"Nothing out of the ordinary. My lawyer had recommended I get things straightened out at home before I do anything else, so I want to run my plans past him first."

"Too bad. I was looking forward to finding you your very own place today."

"We can go later in the week."

They finished breakfast, and Alan left her with a promise to call her that evening.

His mood was grim as he left Tina's apartment to return to his hotel room to get cleaned up. He planned to pay Dorothy a visit that afternoon. He hadn't seen her since the night she'd told him to leave. He wanted to find out what her plans were regarding the house and cars. It wasn't going to be easy seeing her again, and he had to prepare himself for what would undoubtedly be an ugly confrontation.

"I am so excited," Dorothy told Paige. "I've attended your fashion shows before, but I never thought I'd be working at one."

"I'm glad you're here," Paige said. "I need all the help I can get today."

They were rushing around getting Total Elegance ready for the big, festive show scheduled to begin in one hour. The models were due at any minute, the chairs needed to be set up and the refreshments put out. They had already arranged the clothes by their favorite designers neatly in the back by the dressing rooms, so all the models had to do was grab the next outfit on the rack as they returned from the sales floor.

"With any luck, Dorothy, it'll be nonstop action all day," Paige said hopefully.

"And nonstop sales," Dorothy added with a grin.

"I like the way you think, partner!" Paige laughed.

They both looked up as several regular customers entered the store.

"Hi, Paige! We're here for your fashion show," the ladies told them. "But we came early because we wanted to shop before the crowd shows up."

"Enjoy. If you need any help, just let us know."

"We will."

The customers started going through the racks

as Dorothy and Paige put the finishing touches on the modeling area.

Before they knew it, the time had flown by and the models were arriving.

"What would you like me to do?" Dorothy asked, eager to help in any way she could.

"Why don't you cover the floor? If anything comes up that you can't handle, just call me."

"I'll be at the register."

Paige had already trained her on the business side of working in the store, so Dorothy was as ready as she would ever be to face a crowd of excited shoppers.

Tina had expected to spend her entire Saturday with Alan. She'd thought they were going to be apartment hunting, but when he backed out, she was left with the whole day to herself. Tina found she was glad. She needed to have some fun.

Alan had been acting strangely since his run-in with his son and daughter at the office. There was an unspoken tension between them now, and Tina wondered if he was having second thoughts about leaving his wife. The memory of his heated lovemaking convinced her she was worrying for nothing. He still wanted her. There was no doubt about that.

Tina decided to go shopping. She deserved a special treat, and she had noticed a fancy boutique called Total Elegance in town the other day. She'd never shopped there, but it looked like her kind of place—trendy and expensive. She'd seen a sign in the window advertising a fashion show this afternoon, so she decided to attend.

Total Elegance was crowded when Tina arrived. The fashion show was already under way. All the chairs were taken, so she went to stand in the back with the other late arrivals.

The shop was as wonderful as Tina had hoped. She was impressed. The styles were the latest from the established lines, and even featured items from new and upcoming designers. The shop also carried jewelry and other small accessories. Total Elegance was her idea of paradise.

When the show ended, Tina was ready. She'd brought her charge card and intended to make good use of it.

"Is there anything I can help you find today?"

Tina turned and smiled at the young woman who'd offered to wait on her. "Nothing in particular. I'm just going to enjoy myself."

"If you need anything, let me know. I'm Paige."

"I will."

Avid shopper that she was, it wasn't long before Tina had an armful of clothes to try on.

Paige showed her to an empty dressing room, then returned to help Dorothy at the register. The show had been a huge success. They were on their way to having their best day ever.

"The show was wonderful," one of the regular customers complimented Paige as she rang up her purchases.

"We appreciate your coming."

"I wouldn't have missed it." The lady took her

package from Paige and started happily from the store.

"Don't you think she looked a bit like Julia Roberts in *Pretty Woman*?" Dorothy asked after the customer left.

"You know, she did. Smile and all."

Back in the dressing room, Tina tried on all the outfits she'd taken in with her. She fell in love with two of them—a sleek black evening dress that fit her perfectly and showed off every curve, and a trendy business suit. The business suit was serious enough for work, but with the right blouse, Tina knew it could be as enticing as it was professional. She'd found the right blouse, and she was delighted as she waited in line to charge the garments. She couldn't wait to see Alan's reaction when he saw her in the black dress.

"Did you find everything you needed?" Dorothy asked as she took the items from her.

"Oh, yes. You have a wonderful place here. This is my first time in, but I'll be back," Tina promised with a smile.

"I saw you when you came out of the dressing room in this dress," Dorothy said. "It looks fabulous on you."

"Thanks. I have a special someone who's going to appreciate it, too, I think."

They shared a knowing smile.

Dorothy rang up the amounts. She kept the garments on their hangers and covered them with a protective Total Elegance bag before announcing the total.

"Will this be cash or charge?" she asked.

"Charge," Tina answered. She handed her the card.

For a moment, everything was fine.

And then Dorothy looked down and the woman's name struck her.

Tina Lawrence—

A chill swept through Dorothy as she stared down at the charge card.

Keeping her tone conversational even as strange emotions roiled within her, Dorothy was driven to ask, "So, are you new in town, Miss Lawrence?"

"Please, call me Tina, and yes, as a matter of fact, I am new here. I only transferred in a few months ago. I work at Warson-Freeman," she answered. "I'm just sorry it took me so long to find your wonderful store."

Dorothy struggled to keep her outrage under control as she stared down at the printed name.

This was the *Tina!*

Tina noticed a sudden change in her demeanor and wondered at it. "Are you all right?"

"I'm fine." Dorothy turned her back on Tina. "Paige—"

Paige was right there.

"Could you finish this transaction for me?" she asked in a low voice.

"Of course." Paige was confused by her request, but took over smoothly.

Dorothy left the counter and disappeared into the back room without saying another word.

Paige completed the sale and handed the customer the receipt for her signature. "Thank you, Miss"—Paige looked down at her signature—"Lawrence. Come back and see us again."

"I will, and tell your other lady I hope she's feeling better."

When Tina started from the store, Paige went to check on Dorothy. She found her standing in the back room, trembling visibly.

"Dorothy—are you all right?" Paige asked cautiously.

"No." Her answer was quiet, but strained.

That had been Alan's girlfriend—

That had been Tina—

"I have a special someone who's going to appreciate it—"

The younger woman's words echoed in her mind.

At the time, she'd been happy for her.

Now she was filled with rage.

The girl was beautiful—

Young—

Vibrant—

Sexy—

Dorothy bit back a scream of rage at the injustice of it all. Obviously, young Miss Lawrence had no idea whom she'd been talking to, and it was better that way.

"Dorothy—what is it?" Paige pressed her.

Dorothy drew a deep, ragged breath as she looked up at her friend. Paige could see the strain in her expression and the haunted look in her eyes.

"That was her. That was Alan's girlfriend."

Paige immediately went to Dorothy and hugged her. There was nothing she could say to ease her pain. She could only be there for her.

"I didn't know."

"Neither did I until I saw the name on her charge card." Dorothy looked at Paige. "She was buying the dress for 'someone special who was going to appreciate it.'"

"I'm sorry."

"So am I."

"I'd better get back out on the floor. Will you be all right?"

Dorothy nodded. "Is she gone?"

"Yes. She was leaving when I came back here."

"Give me a minute, and I'll be back out to help."

"Are you sure?"

"Absolutely." Dorothy drew on her anger to try to steady herself. "This is our store. We have customers to keep happy."

Tina reached the store's front door just as another young woman was about to enter.

They both stopped, staring at each other in shock through the half-open portal.

"You!" Carol all but shouted at the sight of the woman she despised coming out of Total Elegance. "What are you doing here?"

"I was just leaving," Tina said quickly.

"Good!" Carol snarled.

Tina brushed past her and didn't look back. She wondered what miserable stroke of luck had brought Alan's daughter to that particular store at the particular moment in time. The last thing she wanted was another run-in with her or her brother.

Carol was tempted to say, *Don't let the door hit you in the butt as you leave*, but she controlled the desire. This was Total Elegance—hardly the place for a fight worthy of a pay-per-view wrestling match. She hurried inside to find her mother.

Dorothy had just stepped out of the back room when she saw her daughter coming into the shop. Across the width of the still-crowded room, their gazes met.

Carol knew immediately, just by the look on her mother's face, that she had learned the young woman's identity. She hurried to her side.

"You know?"

"Oh, yes. I was lucky enough to be waiting on her," she said sarcastically. She quickly told Carol what had happened.

"I'm sorry, Mom. I never dreamed anything like this would happen. Did she know who you were?"

"No. I didn't say anything. At least that way, I kept some dignity about me."

"I love you, Mom."

"I love you, too, Carol," she said, appreciating her emotional support. "But I have to get back to work."

Dorothy deliberately lightened her tone and pushed aside all thoughts of Tina Lawrence.

She was a business owner now.

She would concentrate on the store.

Total Elegance would be her lifeline to sanity.

CHAPTER THIRTEEN

"He would be the perfect husband for Christine," Anthony Barrett said with certainty.

"Yes, he would," Laura agreed. "He has money and good looks. It doesn't get any better than that." She looked at her husband. "Just like you, dear."

"Ah, so you only married me for my money and looks?"

"It didn't hurt that I loved you, too, but let's just say your looks and fortune didn't hurt your chances," she laughed.

He laughed, too, then grew a bit serious. "Does Christine love Mark?"

"I honestly don't know," Laura admitted, taking a sip of her strawberry daiquiri.

They were sitting on the dock watching Mark and Christine ride the jet skis.

"He would be a great catch," she said thoughtfully.

"And our daughter would be a great catch for him. They could both do far worse."

"I guess we'll just have to wait and see what happens. I know Margo would be most pleased with a union between them." Laura and Margo met socially on occasion.

"It's their decision to make. No one pushed *us*."

"No one needed to. I knew how wonderful you were without anyone else telling me."

Anthony leaned over and gave his wife of twenty-five years a kiss. "I'm glad I lived up to your expectations."

"Absolutely."

They turned their attention back to the younger couple racing around the lake at top speed.

Christine stopped her jet ski and waited for Mark to come to her side.

"Beat you!" Christine bragged.

"You cheated!" Mark countered.

"I can't help it if you weren't paying attention," she said smugly.

"You want to go again?" he challenged.

"Yes!"

Christine roared off, but this time Mark was ready. He stayed with her. As they made a complete lap of the lake, he passed her and won the race by a good distance.

"All right, I give. You win. Enough racing. Let's go swimming," Christine suggested.

They rode to the dock and tied up the jet skis.

"Having fun, you two?" Laura asked.

"We're going swimming now," Christine told her parents. "You want to come with us?"

"No, we've had about enough sun. We're going back up to the house."

"We'll be up in a while."

Christine and Mark got their beach towels and made their way to the secluded beach area. They spread their towels out on the sand.

"Race you!" Mark started at a run for the water's edge, leaving her to follow.

Christine chased after him and was rewarded by a thorough splashing. "I'll get even with you for that, Mark Seton!"

"What are you going to do?" He backed farther out into the lake until he was standing waist-deep in the water.

"You'll see."

"You have to catch me first."

Christine raced toward him. The water slowed her, but she wasn't one to give up. She was surprised that he made no effort to get away. When she reached him, she threw her arms around his neck and kissed him.

A thrill surged through her at the feel of his hard-muscled chest against her. When he wrapped his arms around her and held her close, she gave a little groan. She had always known that Mark stayed in good shape, but she'd had no idea he was this fit. When she'd seen him in his swimming trunks for the first time, she'd been impressed. It was obvious he was serious about working out. Tall, broad-shouldered and darkly tanned, he didn't have an ounce of spare flesh on him. He looked as good as any of the hunk models on the cover of a body-building magazine. She caressed the width of his shoulders and back as she returned his kiss with fervor. The water lapping around their waists made the embrace that much more sensual.

Mark held Christine close, enjoying their kiss. She was a beautiful woman with a beautiful body. What was not to like? He deepened the kiss, holding her close. He had almost allowed himself to relax and enjoy the pleasure of having her in his arms when she lifted her legs and wrapped them around his waist.

The brazen move shocked Mark. He stepped back deeper into the water and broke off the kiss.

"Your parents—"

"They're up at the house by now. They can't see us here on the beach," Christine said in a sultry, seductive voice.

She kissed him again, passionately. Her kiss told him without words that she wanted him. She moved her hips enticingly against his. As scantily clad as they were in the swimming suits, she could tell Mark was aroused. Christine smiled to herself, glad to know that he wasn't immune to her charms. In all the times they'd dated, he had never been forward with her. Today was the day she planned to change all that.

Mark was aroused. There was no doubt about that. He had been celibate since his breakup with

Jenny, and Christine was an enticing woman. Her kiss was pure excitement, and the feel of her hips moving erotically against his was almost more than he could bear. His animal instincts told him she was offering herself to him—that he should take her and enjoy every minute of it. He was tempted—oh, so tempted to allow himself to be a creature of the flesh, but Mark knew he couldn't.

Not after what had happened with Jenny—

Her image played in his mind and gave him the strength he needed to break off the kiss and put Christine from him.

"Mark?" She was surprised by his action. "Is something wrong?"

"No, nothing's wrong. This just isn't the time or place."

"But I told you—no one can see us," she repeated. She gave him an inviting, sensual smile. She took a step toward him. She wanted to be back in his arms.

"I thought we were going for a swim?" He deliberately turned and swam away from the temptation of her. He knew a good swim would wear him out and take his mind off of what she was blatantly offering him.

Christine was furious and hurt. She had fancied making love to Mark in the water, and on the beach. And then later that night, once her parents had retired, she'd planned to sneak into his room and share his bed until the early morning hours. As Mark swam away, she walked back up on the beach and stretched out on her towel to soak up some rays. She hoped the sight of her lying there would lure him to her side.

Mark caught sight of Christine moving up the beach, and he kept swimming. She had aroused him. He desired her, but he wasn't going to break the vow he'd made to himself all those months ago. What he felt for Christine wasn't love. It was pure animal lust, and he wasn't going to give in to it. The only thing that would help him control his need was exercise and plenty of it. He was going to stay in the water swimming until he was too exhausted to care.

It was a long time before Mark left the water and came to sit on his towel beside Christine.

"Enjoy your swim?" she asked.

"Yes. The water felt great," he answered. He was relieved to be back in control.

"We've got about an hour before I have to go up to the house to get ready. I know you're not Catholic, but we always attend Saturday Mass at St. Gabriel's in town when we're staying at the lodge, and then go out to dinner afterward."

Mark considered making an excuse not to go along. He hadn't been to any church service since he'd ended his relationship with Jenny. Jenny had been very devout, and he had accompanied her to Mass regularly when they were a couple. He'd even considered taking instructions in the faith for a while, but that had been then, and this was now. Mark wasn't sure he was ready to start going to church again, but as a guest of the Barretts, he could hardly refuse.

"That will be fine," Mark said, glad, at least, that they would be in her parents' company for a large portion of the evening.

"Are we ready?" Joe asked the women gathered at his house.

"As we'll ever be," Gail said, smiling brightly.

"This is going to be so much fun!" Eileen said.

"I can't wait to see the look on her face when she answers the door," Audrey agreed.

"All right, let's park at the end of her block. We want this to be as big a surprise as we can pull off," Joe directed.

"If we want to surprise her, we have to sneak up on her," Eileen said.

"You're in charge, Joe. Lead the way."

They started out to the presents-stuffed cars parked in Joe's driveway. Since getting the phone calls the day before, the women had worked furiously to get all the baby items they could for first-time mom Jenny Emerson. Gail had taken charge of the refreshments. Joe had fixed the crib, bought a new mattress for it, and loaded it in the back of his pickup. He had a big bow for it, too, but he wasn't going to put it on until they got to Jenny's. He didn't want it to blow off in traffic.

"We almost look like a caravan," Gail said as they started off down the street.

"Or the Magi arriving early." Joe grinned.

"I'm glad everything worked out so well."

"Jenny is going to be surprised, that's for sure."

It was a short ride, and they all piled out of the cars, eager to start the festivities. Gail led the way to the door carrying the "Happy Baby Shower" sheet cake she'd ordered. Everyone else grabbed as many of the packages as they could carry, and hurried up the sidewalk toward the house.

"I'm ready for some lunch, what about you?" Jenny asked Donna as she put down her paint brush.

"Better late than never," Donna laughed. "It must be almost three o'clock." On a whim, she had stopped by that morning to check on Jenny and had stayed to help her paint the soon-to-be nursery.

They settled in at the kitchen table for a quick sandwich.

"How are you holding up? I don't want you overdoing it."

"I'm tired, but there's nothing new about that."

"Did you have trouble sleeping again?"

"That's normal these days, and I bet I don't get much more rest after the baby's born."

"You're right. All those two-o'clock feedings are going to take their toll."

"Yeah, but I wouldn't have it any other way."

They shared a gentle smile.

"Jenny—" Donna began cautiously. When her friend looked up at her, she went on, "Do you

156

ever think about letting Mark know you're having the baby?"

"Why would I? He made it perfectly clear how he felt about my pregnancy," she said defensively.

"You haven't heard from him at all?"

"No." Jenny almost mentioned seeing him on the street corner the other day, but didn't. There was no point. "He doesn't care about me or this baby. I don't know how I could have been so stupid as to fall in love with someone like him."

"Well, the important thing now is your baby," Donna said to change the topic. Dreamer that she was, she'd always kept hoping that one day Mark would just show up and sweep Jenny off her feet again, but reality had to be faced now. He wasn't coming back, and she supposed that was probably good. Jenny needed someone strong to help her, someone who would put her above the other interests in his life. Mark obviously wasn't that man.

"Yes, he or she is," Jenny said with a smile, resting a hand on her stomach. "So, do you like the mint green?"

"It's perfect. You're going to be safe whether it's a boy or a girl. How are you fixed for baby clothes and diapers?"

Before Jenny could answer, the doorbell rang.

"I wonder who that could be."

"You want me to get it?"

"No, I can."

Jenny got up and made her way slowly toward the front door. She wasn't moving quickly these days, no matter how hard she tried. Through her lace curtains, she could see several people on her porch, and she was surprised. She couldn't imagine who they were.

She opened the door.

"Surprise!" everyone yelled at once.

"What?" Jenny was so shocked, she took a step backward.

"You're having a surprise baby shower," Joe told her, grinning mischievously. "Are you going to let us in or are you going to open presents out here?"

"Oh, Joe—" Tears welled up in Jenny's eyes. "Come in—come in."

She stepped back and watched in complete and utter amazement as the women from church filed in, their arms loaded with presents.

"Where do you want us?" Gail asked.

"The living room is fine," she answered.

They paraded past her as Donna came out of the kitchen.

"What's going on?" she asked, looking from Jenny to the smiling, presents-carrying invaders.

"We're throwing a baby shower!" Gail announced.

Jenny quickly introduced Donna to her friends from church.

"It's lovely to meet you," Eileen said.

"You, too," Donna replied, overwhelmed by the kindness of their actions.

Eileen put down her gifts and started to leave the house, with several other women following her.

"You're not leaving, are you?" Jenny asked. She feared they were going to slip away as quickly as they'd come.

"Oh, no," Eileen and the others answered. "We've got to bring in more presents."

"More?" Jenny repeated, stunned.

"That's right, Jenny. We'll be back in a second."

"Come on now, little girl," Joe said as he took her arm and guided her to a comfortable-looking recliner. "You sit right here and let us take care of everything."

Jenny did as she was told and watched in awe as they spread out the array of presents before her. She'd never dreamed anything like this would happen, and, though she tried to hold them back, she gave in to her tears. "Thank you," she said in an emotional voice.

"You're more than welcome, Jenny," Joe and Gail told her.

"Joe told us you might be short a few things for your baby, so we wanted to help out," Audrey said.

When all the presents had been brought inside and the women had taken seats in the living room and dining room, Eileen urged, "Come on! Start opening your gifts!"

Like a little kid, Jenny started to rip and tear. She exclaimed with delight over each and every present. There were diapers and wipes and outfits and blankets and a music box and a night light and a mobile for a crib and crib sheets. She didn't tell them that she had no crib.

"This is so wonderful! Thank you!"

"And now—" Gail began.

"Now?" Jenny frowned, wondering what could possibly be coming next.

"I'll be right back, but I'll need some help," Joe said.

Three of the women went with him. In no time they were back, half carrying and half rolling the refurbished crib.

"You said the other night that you only had a bassinet, so—"

"Oh, thank you," she breathed, getting up to go embrace each and every one of them.

"We'll get it upstairs for you. Which room is going to be the nursery?" Joe asked.

"It isn't quite finished yet. Donna and I have been working on it all morning."

She led the way upstairs to show them what they'd been doing.

"Why don't we just pitch in and help you finish up?" Joe began rolling up his shirtsleeves. "I'll paint the rest of the room for you. Where did you want the border?"

"Are you sure? Do you have the time?"

"We're not going anywhere until you're all ready for the baby," he said. "Right, ladies?"

"That's right."

"But first—" Gail interrupted.

"What?"

"Cake and ice cream!"

"That's right! We almost forgot!"

160

They all went back downstairs and enjoyed the refreshments. A short time later they were ready.

"Let's get to work," Joe directed. He looked straight at Jenny and ordered, "You get to supervise, so find a chair and keep an eye on us."

She looked up at him, her heart in her eyes. "So, Saint Joseph really is the patron saint of laborers."

"Absolutely," he affirmed with a grin, picking up a paint brush.

"Don't go giving him any big ideas about himself," Gail put in, laughing.

Joe looked at his wife and gave her a mischievous look. "You don't think I'm a candidate for sainthood?"

"Remember who you're talking to, Joe Myers. I'm your wife."

"I'd better get to work."

Everyone laughed as they started in on their labor of love.

CHAPTER FOURTEEN

Mark was impressed by his first view of St. Gabriel's. It was an old church with stained-glass windows and a tall, impressive steeple with a cross on top.

"It's a beautiful church," he told Christine and her parents, pausing on the sidewalk to look up at the building.

"We enjoy coming here. There's something special about the older churches. Our church at home is new and very modern, so this is a treat," Laura said.

Mark followed Christine and her parents up the steps and inside. He was surprised by the sense of peace that enveloped him when he passed through the doors.

It was reverently quiet.

The pews were old.

The ceiling was high, supported by massive pillars.

No one was talking.

Everyone prayed.

Mark followed Christine and her parents up the center aisle to a pew near the front. He slid into the pew next to Christine and sat staring up at the altar, remembering the last time he'd attended a Mass.

It had been with Jenny at her parish in the city.

Mark forced his thoughts away from Jenny. She'd been on his mind too much lately. He tried to focus on the Mass as it began. He listened attentively to the readings and to the Gospel.

Having finished reading the Gospel, the priest announced, "Today we are blessed to have a guest speaker from the archdiocesan office. Charles Wilson is the head of pro-life activities. He's come to talk with us this weekend."

The priest took his seat as Charles Wilson made his way up to the microphone.

"As Father told you, I am the director of the Pro-Life office." He paused and smiled as he looked out across the congregation. "I think it's most appropriate that I'm here, speaking at St. Gabriel's. Gabriel brought the news to Mary that she was with child, and I'm here to bring you news of the pro-life cause—and to make a special request."

Mark immediately, and cynically, assumed Wilson was going to hit everyone up for money. He had no doubt that in a few minutes they'd be passing the basket, seeking donations. He was prepared to completely ignore anything the man had to say. Life was all about money. His mother had taught him that. When the basket came his way, he'd put a few dollars in just so no one thought he was cheap, but he wasn't interested in the man's message.

"Life is love," Charles Wilson declared with certainty. "It's as simple as that—and as complicated. God created us to be loving creatures. Jesus said, 'Love one another as I have loved you.' So often during the course of our days, we lose track of the meaning of our existence. So many other things can intrude and distract us from our purpose in life. We need to concentrate on what is really important—and what is really important is to love and nurture each other from the moment of conception until death. Life is our most precious gift. We need to treasure it. At the end of the pews on the side aisles you will find—"

Here it comes, Mark thought sarcastically. *No doubt there are envelopes at the end of the pews to put the money in.*

"Prayer cards."

Mark was surprised.

"All we are asking from you are your prayers for the sanctity of life. Please pass the cards down the pew so everyone can have one to keep."

Mark took the card Christine passed to him and glanced down at it.

There on the prayer card was the very real image of an unborn child sucking its thumb.

In that instant, Jenny was back in his thoughts. He remembered all too clearly the wondrous look on her face when she'd told him she was pregnant with their child.

She had been so excited.

She had thought it was good news.

Their son—their daughter—he remembered how she'd used those terms so openly and with such pride.

Mark continued to stare down at the picture for a moment longer. But there was no child now. Jenny had told him she'd taken care of it.

A sudden jarring guilt swept through him. Was he responsible for what had happened to their child? His mother had argued that it wasn't a child yet.

Mark scowled and forced the memory of that traumatic time away. He took one last look at the card. Disturbed by the image, he put it, picture side down, on the pew next to him.

Mark was glad when the Mass was over and they started to file out of the pew.

He wanted to distance himself from the church. He did not take the prayer card.

There was no easy escape for Mark, though. Just before he left the church, he came face-to-face with a painting depicting St. Gabriel and Mary in the Annunciation. Mark hurried on.

"It's perfect!" Jenny said in pure delight as she stared around the nursery.

The painting was done. The crib had been

brought upstairs and set up with the new musical mobile attached. The curtains had been hung, and all the baby clothes she'd received as gifts that day had been laundered, neatly folded and put away in the dresser drawers. With the help of several of the women, Joe had managed to move the unwanted furniture to the basement, so the house was as ready as it would ever be for Jenny's new addition.

"You like it?" Gail asked.

"I love it! Thank you! Thank you all!" Jenny made the circle of the room, hugging and kissing everyone. "And look how fast we did it. It's amazing! You're amazing—"

"No, Jenny," Audrey said quietly. "You're amazing."

"Is there anything else you need right now?" Eileen asked.

"I can't imagine," Jenny replied, completely humbled by their generosity. "You've taken care of everything!"

"Well, if you think of anything, you just let one of us know," Eileen insisted.

"How can I ever repay you?" Jenny asked sincerely.

"I know! You can buy me the winning Power Ball ticket," Joe teased. "Just think how much good we could do if we had all that money to work with."

Everyone laughed in good humor. They all knew it wasn't the money that had made this day special. It was the love.

"We love you, Jenny. You don't owe us a thing. You just take care of yourself and that baby," Joe told her. He kissed her cheek.

"I will."

"What Mass are you going to tomorrow?" Gail asked.

"Probably ten-thirty. Why?"

"That's when we always go, so we'll see you then."

They started to leave. Jenny and Donna followed the loving group out onto the porch to wave good-bye. Joe and Gail were the last to drive off. As Jenny watched them go by in the pickup, the baby gave a strong, enthusiastic kick.

She got the message.

She smiled.

She would ask Joe and Donna to be her baby's godparents.

Joe was feeling good as he drove back to their house. "It went well, don't you think?"

"It was wonderful," Gail agreed. "I'm just so sorry things didn't work out for her with Mark."

"I know. A baby needs both his mother and his father."

"I did talk to Jenny's friend Donna about him."

"What did she say?"

"She didn't say a lot, but she believes Jenny still cares for him. There was some kind of trouble between them when she found out she was pregnant, and that was when she broke up with him."

"So she ended the relationship—"

"According to Donna."

Joe fell silent, lost in deep thoughts.

Christine's parents retired to their private quarters shortly after returning from having dinner in town, leaving Christine and Mark together.

The evening stretched endlessly before Mark. He wanted to leave. He didn't exactly know why he was so uncomfortable with Christine right now, he just was. He needed to get away, to have some time alone so he could think.

"Want to go out on the deck?" Christine suggested.

"Sure."

Mark followed her outside, and they sat on a cushioned two-seater swing.

It was going to be a beautiful, clear night. The sun was setting, its fading light painting the western horizon a myriad of pinks and purples and reds.

"If an artist painted a picture like this, no one would believe it could be real," Mark remarked, staring up at the sky.

"God is a fantastic artist."

"You're right. I hadn't thought of Him that way before."

"God has to be a right-brainer. Look how creative He is," Christine joked.

"Seven days for everything—not too bad," Mark agreed.

"What's your favorite thing God created?" Christine asked, leaning a little closer as she gazed up at Mark. Her expression was one of open adoration as she awaited his answer.

"Fast cars," he answered. The only real pleasure he found in life now was getting out on the highway and taking off, just driving as fast as he could, as far as he could. Driving was his only escape. "What about you?"

Christine fought to hide her disappointment at Mark's answer. She had hoped he would say *she* was. She decided to be brazen in responding to him, hoping he would come to realize she wanted to deepen their relationship. "You are," she said softly.

Mark was surprised by her words and even more surprised by her actions. Before he could respond, she lifted her lips to his and kissed him hungrily, looping her arms around his neck and pressing herself against him in a blatant sensual offering.

Mark accepted her kiss. Christine was a lovely woman. He liked her as a person, but he did not desire her. Caught up in a difficult situation, he had never been so glad to hear his cell phone ring as he was just then.

Christine couldn't believe her rotten luck. She'd finally gotten Mark alone, and his phone had to ring! She managed a tight smile as they broke apart.

"Excuse me for a minute," Mark told her, standing and moving a few steps away to take the call.

Christine couldn't help listening to his conversation. She didn't want to eavesdrop, but when someone was standing so close by, there was no way to completely ignore what they were saying.

"I understand," Mark said, his tone serious. "There isn't any other way to handle it?"

He waited as the other person spoke.

"I see. All right."

He stopped again, listening intently. He looked at his wristwatch.

"If there's no other way, I can be back in the city in about two hours. Is that good enough?"

He paused.

"All right. I'll see you then." He ended the conversation and turned to Christine. "You heard?"

"Do you really have to go?" She was incredulous.

"Yes. That was my mother. There's some kind of last-minute trouble with one of the new contracts she negotiated, and she needs me at the office as soon as I can get there." Mark remained standing a distance away from her.

Christine stood up and went to him. "You can't wait until tomorrow morning?"

"She's at the office waiting for me right now."

Mark did not want to appear too eager to leave, so he drew her close and kissed her gently. "I'm sorry I have to go, but there's no way out of it."

"I'll go tell my parents. They'll want to see you off."

They walked back inside together. He went to his room to pack while she went to get her mother and father. A short time later they were all standing in front of the lodge.

"Thank you so much for your hospitality. I'm sorry I have to leave so soon," Mark said as he shook her father's hand.

"I understand, Mark. Sometimes business does intrude," Anthony said. He was a successful businessman. He knew that when duty called, everything else had to be put aside.

"Give your mother our best," Laura added. "And please, plan to join us again. It was delightful having you here."

"It was my pleasure," he answered. Looking at Christine, he smiled at her. "I'll talk with you this week."

"I'll be waiting."

Mark made no move to kiss her good-bye, so she stood back to watch as he drove away.

Mark waved once, then turned his concentration to driving. He had never before been so glad to hear from his mother as he had been this evening. What Christine didn't know was that his mother had called merely to ask how he was doing on his weekend with the Barretts. She had hung up before he'd said that he would return to the city.

There was no pressing problem at the office.

There was no emergency.

The only emergency facing Mark was saving himself.

And he'd done it.

Joe was alone in his study. It was late, well past ten, and he still hadn't made his final decision.

Should he call Mark Seton or not?

A part of Joe believed it was the right thing to do. If, as Gail had mentioned, Jenny did still love him and would soon be giving birth to his child, Mark should know.

Joe stared down at Mark Seton's number in the phone book, open in front of him on his desk. He mumbled a quick prayer that he was doing the right thing, then dialed Mark's number.

The phone rang endlessly.

Joe was about to hang up when the answering machine came on.

Joe had been debating all evening exactly what to say if he was able to reach Mark.

He left a quiet, anonymous message. "It's important for you to see Jenny now."

Joe hung up and offered up another quick prayer that he'd done the right thing.

CHAPTER FIFTEEN

It was late.

Dorothy lay in bed staring at the ceiling, wondering if her life could possibly get any more miserable. She still had trouble believing Tina had actually come into Total Elegance that afternoon. The day had been going so well, and then—

Tossing restlessly, Dorothy sought sleep, but sleep would not come. Her mind was too active. All she could think about was Alan—and that girl.

And Tina *was* a girl.

She was young—and beautiful.

Dorothy had actually liked talking to Tina and enjoyed waiting on her until she'd learned who she was.

As she felt herself starting to cry again, Dorothy finally got angry. She would not allow herself to care about Alan anymore. As long as she cared, she could be hurt. From this moment on, she would deny any and all affection for the father of her children.

True, their marriage had been a good one while it lasted. She had raised two wonderful children. She now had a perfect grandson, thanks to Carol and her husband. She had had the opportunity to do a lot of good work volunteering, too, since she'd had no need to hold down a paying job.

But those days were over now.

Her future was very different from what she'd thought it would be. She had a new life now. She was a businesswoman, and she fully intended to be successful. With her social connections, she firmly believed she could boost Total Elegance's sales. It was just a matter of working hard and getting the word out about the shop to her well-to-do friends.

Work was going to be her saving grace. She would never be able to forget what had happened, but she could become a strong and independent woman who didn't need anyone, least of all Alan. She was making a new life for herself, and she was determined that it was going to be a wonderful life.

Silently Dorothy offered up a prayer for God's guidance.

It was one thing to start a new life at fifty-something. It was another to be brave about it.

Dorothy was certain her guardian angel was working overtime.

Mark reached his apartment and tossed his car keys on the kitchen counter. He took a quick look at the answering machine to find there were five new messages. It was an easy decision to ignore them as he headed for the shower. Tomorrow would be soon enough to worry about who was trying to reach him. He was certain the messages were all business-related anyway.

The drive home had helped Mark relax, and he was feeling much better as he got ready to call it a night. He had no plans for Sunday, and he was glad. It was a rare day when he wasn't under some kind of pressure at work. After closing the big deal last week, he figured he owed himself a little peace and quiet.

Monday was going to come all too soon. He intended to enjoy Sunday.

Darrell was miserable as he sat alone in the darkened living room with only the TV set on. Claire had gone to bed some time ago, which was just as well. He didn't want her to see him so tense and on edge. Every time he heard a car drive by, he expected trouble. He'd turned out all the lights and had drawn the drapes, but his precautions hadn't helped to ease his fears. He felt impotent and helpless, and that didn't sit well with him.

Darrell lifted his beer and took a deep drink. He'd already finished off a six-pack, and he was ready for more. When he got drunk enough, he could forget the horror his life had become. He'd thought he was done with all the ugliness when he'd walked out of prison after paying his dues. He'd decided to put his other life behind him and try to make it in the real world. He'd wanted to do it for Claire. She had stayed by him during his jail time. She had never lost faith in him. He loved her.

Darrell took another swig of beer. He was furious at his vulnerability. He couldn't do anything to help himself. He was totally unprotected, a sitting duck. The cops had said they'd help, but what could they do?

Looking around the room, Darrell finally knew what he needed to do. He needed to get a gun. He needed to go find those low-life bastards and take care of them himself.

To hell with relying on the cops to keep Claire safe.

He was her man.

He should do it.

Darrell made up his mind as he finished his beer. He was ready to get up and leave the apartment. To find someone selling a hot gun on the street and go looking for trouble, before trouble came looking for him.

"Darrell?" Claire called his name from the bedroom doorway. She'd fallen asleep while waiting for him to join her, and had just awakened to find he still wasn't there.

"What?" He jumped nervously and looked in Claire's direction. As dark as his thoughts had been, her interruption was a shock.

"I thought you were coming to bed."

"I can't sleep."

"Why don't you come and lie down with me?

You can watch TV in the bedroom. You don't have to sit in here all by yourself." Claire saw all the empty beer cans by his chair and knew he was drunk. She wished there was some way she could make everything right again for him, but she couldn't. Nothing would be the same until the police found and arrested the men who did the shooting.

"No. I was just thinking of going out for a while." He stood up.

"Why? There's nowhere to go tonight. Come to bed."

"You don't understand. I got something I have to take care of." He sounded harsh.

"What?" she demanded, fearing what he was about to do. She knew what the consequences might be if he tried to go after the gunman himself.

"None of your business, woman."

"Don't talk to me like that," she said, coming to stand before him. "I don't want you going out. Who knows what could happen to you?"

"I plan to make sure nothing happens—to me or to you," he told her.

She looked up at Darrell and saw the fierce torment in his expression. "Baby, I love you. Don't even think about doing this—"

"They have to be stopped, and I have to do it."

"You did your part by telling the police. They'll catch the killers. I know they will."

"You have more faith in the cops than I do." He sounded disgusted.

"Darrell, listen to me. It's only been a couple

days. Give them time." She reached up and touched his cheek, forcing him to look down at her. "We've been through so much, just so we could be together. Stay here with me. I need you. I love you."

Darrell gazed down at Claire, seeing her beauty and her innocence. She meant the world to him. He was torn by his conflicting emotions. "But I have to keep you safe."

She kissed him. It was a gentle, loving kiss that spoke more of devotion than animal passion. "As long as I'm in your arms, I am safe. Don't leave me again, Darrell. Please."

She kissed him again. It was a desperate emotional plea.

This time he responded fully, telling her with his embrace that she was his life—his love.

"Let's go to bed," Claire whispered.

He nodded. Any idea of returning to his old way of life was banished by the power of her pure love.

They moved together into the bedroom and made passionate, desperate love. When their frantic emotions had been spent, they lay together, wrapped in each other's arms.

"Darrell, let's go to your church in the morning," Claire said softly.

"You want to go to church?" He was surprised. She had never spoken of attending church before.

"Yes. You've talked so much about Our Lady lately, I want to go. I've been past it hundreds of times, but I've never been inside."

"But tomorrow is Sunday."

"Yes. So? Isn't that when we're supposed to go?"

"I've never been there on a Sunday."

"Then it's time to start, don't you think?"

Darrell was surprised by her suggestion, but in a way he was very glad, too. When he stopped at Our Lady on his way home from work every morning, he felt protected for the day, as if God's grace was surrounding him. More than once, he'd wondered if God was calling him—if God wanted him to join the church. Somehow it seemed very right, but he was still a little cautious about making any definite commitment just yet. He had plenty of time to make up his mind. He'd lived this long without belonging to any church. There was no reason to rush into anything.

"All right. We'll go."

"When are the services? Do you know?"

"I think the sign out front says there's an eight-thirty, a ten-thirty and a twelve o'clock Mass."

"Let's go at ten-thirty. It'll be the most crowded, so it will be the safest."

"And it will also mean we can sleep a little later."

"That's right." Claire gave a throaty laugh. "Do you plan on keeping me awake tonight?"

Darrell bent over her and kissed her.

Claire linked her arms around his neck and drew him down to her. She did love this man. In her heart, she prayed that God would guide them.

Alan had tried to catch up with Dorothy all day, but she hadn't been at home. In frustration, he had finally gone by the house to leave her a note, telling her he needed to talk to her, only to discover his key didn't work.

Dorothy had changed the locks.

Rage had filled him.

Alan's mood had still been dark when he'd gone to pick up Tina, and it hadn't improved when she'd mentioned her encounter with his daughter that afternoon at the boutique. He'd made his excuses for not staying the night with her and had dropped her at her apartment and returned to his hotel room. She hadn't been happy about it. Amazingly, he hadn't cared.

Alan was angry as he lay in his solitary bed, trying to understand what had happened to his life. Nothing was going right. A few days earlier, he'd been happy with his decision to leave Dorothy. He'd thought his future with Tina would be exciting, but the only excitement he'd had so far had been a nasty altercation with his son and daughter and discovering his checking accounts had been emptied and the locks changed.

That wasn't the kind of excitement he'd been expecting.

CHAPTER SIXTEEN
DAY SIX

Lord, Give Me Hope . . .

Joe had passed an uneasy night. He felt he'd done the right thing, leaving the message on Mark Seton's answering machine. He just hoped Mark was moved by it and contacted Jenny.

As he lay in bed in the pre dawn hours, Joe offered up a prayer for Mark and Jenny. The way things looked, it would take a miracle to bring the two of them together again.

But that realization didn't disturb Joe.

Miracles were what God did best.

Mark woke up early but didn't immediately get out of bed. It felt good doing nothing for a while. Eventually, though, the sunshine got the best of him. He was a morning person. He got up.

Showered, shaved and dressed, Mark made his way to the kitchen to see what he could eat for breakfast. He opened the refrigerator door and discovered the pickings were slim. He didn't keep a lot of food around because he wasn't home that much, but there was a carton of orange juice and half a loaf of bread. He dined happily on toast and juice while he read the newspaper.

It was after ten A.M. when Mark finally decided he was ready to listen to the messages on his answering machine. He pressed the play button and listened to the messages. The first three were from Joanne, updating him on things at the office. He deleted them all. The fourth was from his mother, as he'd expected, asking him to call her when he returned from the Barretts' lodge. He deleted it, too.

And then he played the last message.

"It's important for you to see Jenny now."

Mark froze and stared down at the answering machine in disbelief. He hit the play button again and stood, listening.

"It's important for you to see Jenny now."

Mark did not recognize the man's voice.

He frowned.

Jenny—

She had haunted him all weekend and now this—

It's important for you to see Jenny now.

Suddenly Mark knew what he had to do. He had to find Jenny. He had to see her and talk to her and find out how she was. If he missed her this much, maybe she was missing him, too.

It was a slim hope, he realized, remembering their last conversation and how they'd parted, but it was a hope nonetheless. The time he'd spent with Christine had only reaffirmed how deep his feelings were for Jenny, even after all the months of being apart.

Mark glanced at the clock and saw it was after ten. Since it was Sunday, he knew she'd be going to church, but he had no idea which Mass she attended. He decided to stop by her house first. If she wasn't there, he'd head for Our Lady.

Jenny awoke early and faced Sunday morning happier than she had been in ages. She realized that God really did take care of you, if you trusted in Him. Except for Donna's friendship, her life had seemed empty for a long time now. Because of the kindness and generosity of Joe and Gail and the ladies from church, she suddenly realized how truly blessed she was. She got dressed for church and headed off, eager to see her friends again, and eager to tell God, "Thanks."

Claire and Darrell arrived a few minutes early for 10:30 Mass. A good crowd was there already, but they managed to find seats near the front. They knelt down before entering the pew as they'd watched others do and then sat quietly together, offering up their own silent prayers.

Darrell had a hangover. His head was pounding. He was tempted to pray for it to go away, but he knew it was his own fault. He shouldn't have gotten so drunk last night. At the time, it had seemed the only thing he could do. He was sick of feeling helpless. He wanted control over his own life. He wanted to feel like a man again.

The pregnant woman Darrell had seen at the 6:30 weekday Mass entered the pew ahead of them. She nodded to him, smiling, before kneeling and turning her attention to prayer.

Darrell looked around and saw several people he recognized from the weekday Mass. It gave him a comfortable feeling to know he wasn't surrounded by strangers. Not that they knew each other, but there was some kind of comfort in knowing they were there.

Dorothy sat near the front as she always did. She usually came to Mass with a warm and loving heart, but this morning anger was still driving her. She questioned God's plan for her life and what her future held. She kept praying for guidance or for some sign that she was doing the right thing. It seemed to Dorothy, though, that her prayers were being answered with silence. She was sullen as the Mass started.

It was well past 10:30 when Mark reached Our Lady. Jenny hadn't been at home, so he'd come to the church to see if he could find her. He slipped in the side door and sat in one of the back pews, looking around for her. He thought he caught a glimpse of Jenny sitting up front, but he couldn't be sure. The pews ahead of him were full and blocked his view.

Mark made his plan. When it came time for

Communion, he would leave the church and wait outside. Jenny always exited by the front door. If she was there, he would find her.

It's important for you to see Jenny now.

Mark's gaze was drawn back time and again in the direction of the woman he thought was Jenny.

Who had left the message?

And why?

Mark forced himself to bide his time. This was the closest he had been to her in months. Soon he would be talking with her again. It wasn't going to be easy, but that message on his answering machine wouldn't let him back down.

He wanted to be here.

He wanted to see her.

Everyone stood up. The priest began reading the Gospel. Mark recognized the passage from the night before. He wondered if there was going to be a pro-life speaker at this Mass as there had been at St. Gabriel's.

"The Gospel of the Lord," Father Walters intoned when he finished the reading.

"Praise to you, Lord Jesus Christ," everyone responded.

Everyone sat down to await his sermon.

Father Walters looked out over the congregation. "As Catholics, we should have no doubt that life begins at conception. Each unborn child is special. I'm sure most of you have seen the ultrasound picture of the unborn baby sucking his thumb. Now, I have a new photo to tell you about. Not long ago, a surgeon was operating on an unborn baby to correct a condition called spina bifida. When the doctor had finished the procedure and was preparing to close the incision in the womb, the baby stuck his arm out and grasped the doctor's finger. We have flyers in the vestibule with the picture on it, along with the prayer we ask you to pray and meditate on this week."

The sermon only reinforced the uneasiness that had troubled Mark since attending St. Gabriel's. Cynically he realized he would definitely have been more comfortable if they had just asked for money as he'd first suspected the night before.

When it came time for those in his pew to go to Communion, Mark left. He was crossing the vestibule when he saw that one of the flyers the priest had talked about had fallen to the floor. Mark did not stop to pick it up. He kept going, but he did not look away quickly enough to avoid seeing the unforgettable image there.

Mark waited at the bottom of the front steps for Jenny to appear. He had a good view of the front doors and would be able to spot her the minute she came out. He wasn't sure exactly what he would say to her when they finally came face-to-face. It had been so long since they'd been together, since they'd talked. The memory of seeing her on the bus the other day only reaffirmed his need to see her. He waited, tense and uncertain.

Jenny waited until the choir had stopped singing and Father Walters had gone out into the vestibule before leaving her pew. As she did, the man she knew only from 6:30 Mass was exiting his pew, too.

"It's good to see you this morning," Jenny greeted him.

"It's good to see you, too," Darrell responded.

"You're new to the parish, aren't you?"

"Yes, we are," he answered.

"Well, I'm Jenny Emerson."

"I'm Darrell Miller, and this is Claire."

"It's nice to finally get the chance to speak to you. We're always in such a hurry on weekdays."

"Working does that to you."

"Yes, it does," she agreed.

Darrell waited for Jenny to pass by before following with Claire.

Jenny reached the end of the aisle and saw Joe and Gail off to the side of the vestibule. She hurried over to speak with them.

"Good morning," Joe said with a big smile.

"Yes, it is," Jenny agreed.

"You look beautiful today," Gail said, thinking Jenny had an absolute glow about her.

Jenny could only laugh. "I don't feel very beautiful. I only feel big."

"Isn't there a slogan—Big Is Beautiful?" Joe quipped.

"They must have been thinking of me when they made it up!"

"How are you feeling this morning?" Gail asked, concerned.

"I'm fine. I was looking at the nursery again this morning, and it is absolutely perfect. Thank you."

"We love you," Joe answered simply. "If you need anything else, you just let us know."

"I do need something," she said in a very serious tone.

Joe looked immediately worried. "What is it?"

"I need a hug from both of you."

Joe and Gail laughed, their concern eased as they each gave her a warm hug.

"You stay out of trouble, little girl," Joe said in his fatherly tone.

"I'll try."

Jenny was smiling as she started from the church, one of the last to leave.

Joe stood with Gail, watching Jenny walk away. He'd been keeping an eye out for Mark Seton all morning, but he hadn't seen any sign of him. He hoped his message had reached Mark. There wasn't much more he could do right now but pray for Jenny and her baby.

"Are you all right? You look worried about something," Gail said, eyeing her husband suspiciously. When Joe got that particular look on his face, he was usually up to something.

"No, I'm not worried about anything. Come on. Let's go home. I'm ready for some breakfast."

They left by the side door.

Joe did not see Mark waiting impatiently by the front steps.

Mark was almost ready to give up his vigil. He had just about convinced himself that it hadn't been Jenny he'd seen inside. Frustrated, he was about to turn away when the main door opened one more time.

And Jenny walked out.

Mark stared up at her in absolute silence as shock radiated through him at the sight of her.

Jenny was still pregnant!

CHAPTER SEVENTEEN

The thought, *Is it mine?* echoed in Mark's mind, and he immediately hated himself for even thinking it.

He knew the answer.

Of course it is.

Jenny hadn't had the abortion!

She is having my baby!

Mark couldn't speak. He couldn't move. He could only stand there watching her as she started slowly down the steps.

Jenny sensed someone was watching her.

She stopped to look up.

It was then that she saw him, and her blood ran cold.

What is Mark doing here?

She wanted to break and run, but there was nowhere to go, and besides she couldn't have run anyway. She just stood stock-still, staring at him.

Mark saw the mix of wild emotions playing in her expression as their gazes met.

"Hello, Jenny," he said, his voice low and husky with emotion.

"What are you doing here?" Panic was eating at her. This wasn't supposed to be happening.

"I came to see you."

"Why?" she challenged angrily.

"Jenny—I—" He looked around, uncomfortable with having this discussion in public. "Is there someplace we can go to talk?"

"I don't have anything to say to you," she ground out. For all the last endless months, she had ached to see Mark again. She wanted him with her, needed him by her side. But he had never come to her, and she finally realized she was being ridiculous. Mark didn't care about her, and he certainly didn't care about their child.

"But you're having my child," he said quietly, his gaze going over her.

"I'm having *my* child."

"This is my baby, too."

"Now it's your baby," she said sarcastically. "Not so long ago 'it' was a problem that needed to be taken care of."

"I was wrong," he admitted. "I want to do my part."

"You did your part when you sent that check— you and your mother," she answered coldly. "You gave up all rights to my baby. I told you not to call me anymore, and I meant it. Go away and stay away."

"Jenny, please." Mark closed the distance between them. He stood before her, his gaze meeting and holding hers. He lifted one hand to touch her cheek.

"Go away." She ducked her head to avoid his touch. "I don't need you or your money."

"I'm sorry, Jenny. I never meant to hurt you. I love you."

"How can you even say that?" She looked at him, shocked by his declaration. "I thought you were the most wonderful man in the world! I loved you. I believed you when you said we would be together forever." Deep anguish choked her.

"I said that because it's the truth, but this isn't the place for this conversation. Come to my apartment with me—"

"No!" The last thing she wanted was to be alone with him in his apartment, the very place where they'd laughed and loved.

"Then I'll come to your house with you."

She stared up at him, confused and troubled by his unexpected intrusion in her life.

"Why are you here?" Her words were almost a whisper.

"Because I needed to see you. I had to see you. Please—can't we go someplace where we can talk privately?"

A part of Jenny wanted to run away from Mark and never look back, but another long-denied part of her ached to go back into what had once been the safe haven of his arms. Jenny hated herself for feeling that way about him. He had wanted her to get rid of their child.

And now he was back.

Confusion tore at her, but she finally relented. "All right. We can go to my house."

"My car is—"

"You can drive if you want. I'm walking. You know where I live. I'll meet you there." She didn't want to sit in a car with him. She didn't want to be that physically close to him.

Mark was surprised she refused his offer of a ride. "I'll walk with you."

Jenny shrugged and started off. Mark didn't hesitate. He stayed right by her side. Neither of them spoke.

It was only a few blocks to Jenny's house, but that morning it seemed the longest walk she'd ever taken in her life. When they finally reached the steps to the porch, Mark tried to take her arm.

"I don't need your help. I'm pregnant. I'm not an invalid." She shrugged off his touch.

"You're a very brave woman, Jenny."

She glanced at him in amazement as she paused to unlock the door. "You think I'm not afraid? I'm terrified at the thought of having a child and raising it without a father."

She opened the door and went in. Mark followed her.

"He has a father."

"No." Her expression was serious. "He doesn't."

"My name will be on the birth certificate."

"Not unless I put it there."

"This child is mine."

"No. I told you, as far as I'm concerned, you gave up your rights. This child is mine."

"Jenny, this baby is mine, and we both know it. I want a chance—a chance to prove to you how sorry I am."

She turned her back on him and walked into the living room. Her emotions were in an upheaval. Mark followed her into the room. When Jenny sat down on the sofa, he remained standing.

"Not a day has gone by when you weren't on my mind. I want to be a part of your life—of our baby's life." He paused until she looked up at him. "I love you, Jenny. It's taken me this long to realize what I threw away. After I saw you on the bus the other day, all I could think about was you. I want us to be together."

Jenny heard the depth of emotion in his voice, and she closed her eyes. For so long she had prayed for this moment, and now it was really happening.

Her prayers had been answered.

Mark had come to her.

But instead of joy, she felt only anger. The months of her pregnancy had been torture—worrying if she was doing the right thing, trying to decide whether to raise her baby alone or put it up for adoption. All that time could have been wonderful—if they'd been together.

"Are you all right?" Mark asked, troubled by her cool reaction.

"I can't forget the pain, Mark," she answered,

looking up at him. "I can't just pretend nothing's happened."

"I'm not asking you to." He was serious. "I realize now how wrong I was."

She looked up at him, her eyes narrowing as she remembered all too clearly his mother's interference in their relationship. "What about your mother? You know how she feels about me."

"I'll handle my mother."

"Like you did last time?" Jenny couldn't hide the disgust she was feeling.

"No," Mark said. "I'll handle her."

He had never been more serious. This woman meant the world to him. Somehow he had to convince her of the truth of his feelings. He had made a serious mistake all those months ago. He had listened to his mother, not to his heart. He was ready to atone for what he'd done. He was ready to spend the rest of his life making it up to Jenny—if she would let him.

Jenny looked up at the man she was afraid to let back in her world.

When she didn't respond, he added, "Trust me, Jenny. No one is going to come between us again. No one. If you want me to walk away from Seton Leasing, quit my job, I will." He knew that as long as he worked there, his mother would have a way to control him. If giving up his job was what it took to win Jenny back, he would do it.

"We'll see," was all she could say.

Jenny couldn't let herself trust Mark again.

Not yet.

* * *

Alan had considered going to Mass but decided against it. He'd been raised Catholic, and his sense of guilt was well developed. Dorothy would be at 10:30 Mass this morning, he had no doubt about that, so he drove to the house after eleven and waited in his car in the driveway for her return. He hoped she didn't linger at Our Lady too long. He had promised Tina he would pick her up at one and he didn't want to be late. She hadn't been very happy with him when he'd left her last night, and he didn't want to make the tension between them any worse. He'd promised her a big day today, and he intended to keep that promise.

At the sound of a car coming, Alan looked up and saw Dorothy turning in to the driveway. She pulled up alongside him to park. He girded himself for what was to come and got out of the car to face her for the first time in days.

Dorothy was surprised to find Alan at the house waiting for her. A part of her was glad to see him, but it was a very small part. Mostly, she wished he'd stayed away. She grabbed up her purse and climbed out of her car.

"What do you want?" Dorothy demanded, in no mood for small talk.

"We need to talk."

"Call my lawyer."

"I'm serious." He came around his car.

"So am I." She walked right past him on her way to the back door.

"Why did you change the locks?"

199

"To keep you out," she answered simply as she started up the back-porch steps. "Good-bye, Alan. Go away. I'm sure your girlfriend wants to see you. I don't."

"Dorothy—" he began.

She ignored him as she unlocked the door.

"The phone—" She heard the phone ringing and wanted to hurry to get it.

As she let herself in, Alan stepped up and pushed his way inside with her.

"What do you think you're doing?" She ran for the phone, giving him a dirty look.

"I told you—we need to talk."

"Hello?" Dorothy deliberately turned her back on him to concentrate on her phone call.

Alan was glad to be in the house. He sat down at his usual seat at the kitchen table to wait while she finished the conversation.

"What? When?" Dorothy asked quickly.

Alan heard the concern in her tone and wondered what was going on. He glanced up at her and immediately knew something was terribly wrong by the look on her face.

"All right. I'll be right there. Your father is here with me. I'll tell him for you so you don't have to worry about it." She paused to listen, then answered, "I have no idea why he's here or what he wants. He was waiting for me after church, and we haven't had time to talk yet."

She was quiet again.

"I'll see you in a minute. 'Bye." Dorothy hung up and faced Alan.

"What happened?"

"That was Carol. They had to rush the baby to the hospital."

"Why?" he asked, concerned about their six-month-old grandson, Nick.

"Nick's running a high fever, and he had a seizure. They're in the emergency room right now. I'm going."

"I'll go with you."

"Whatever." She rushed from the house.

"I can drive us both, if you want."

"Fine." She locked the door to the house behind them once he was out.

They climbed into his car and drove off. Neither spoke on the drive.

As soon as Alan had pulled into a parking place in the emergency-room lot, Dorothy was out of the car, rushing toward the door. By the time Alan came inside, she was already at the main desk, talking to a nurse.

"If you'll have a seat in the waiting area, I'll see what I can find out for you," the nurse told her.

They moved off to await her return.

Dorothy was relieved to see several other people in the waiting area. She didn't particularly want to talk to Alan. She supposed it was good that he cared enough about Nick to have come to the hospital, but she really didn't want to be around him. She realized it didn't really matter what she wanted or didn't want. All that mattered was Nick. She waited nervously, jumping a bit every time someone entered the room.

"Mom—" Carol appeared in the doorway.

At the sight of her daughter looking so distraught, Dorothy rushed to give her a hug. "How is Nick?"

"Yes, how is he?" Alan asked. He'd been standing on the far side of the room.

Carol was surprised to see him. "You're here—"

"Of course I'm here. Where else would I be?"

She looked back to her mother. "He's running a high fever and they're doing tests right now. I don't know any more than that."

"Is he awake?"

"Off and on. He's a very sick little boy."

"They don't have any idea what's wrong?" Alan pressed.

"Not yet. I'll come and tell you the minute I hear something."

"I'll be right here," Dorothy reassured her.

"Me, too," Alan added.

"Is there anything you need? Anything I can do to help?" Dorothy asked.

Carol looked at her mother desperately. "Pray. Please, pray."

Dorothy nodded and gave her a quick kiss on the cheek. "I will."

Carol rushed off to rejoin her husband, who was keeping vigil at the baby's bedside.

Dorothy glanced toward Alan. "I'm going to the chapel for a while."

"I'll be along in a minute. I have to make a call."

She knew exactly whom he was going to call,

and she didn't care if he came to the chapel or not. She only cared about finding a quiet place to pray for Nick.

Alan went out to the car and got his cell phone. He had been due to pick up Tina at one and he was late already.

"Hello," Tina answered.

"Tina, it's me. Something has come up—"

Before he could say any more she interrupted him.

"Where are you, Alan? I've been waiting for you." Her irritation was evident in her voice.

"I'm at the hospital."

In an instant, her tone changed. "Are you all right?"

"I'm fine, but my grandson is ill."

"What's wrong with him?"

He had mentioned Nick to her on several occasions, but she'd never seen the child, and, frankly, she didn't care to. She didn't like to think of Alan as a grandfather.

"They don't know yet. They're doing tests."

"Well, why don't you just have them call you on your cell phone when they get the results?" It seemed very simple to Tina.

"I can't leave, Tina."

"Why not?"

"I have to be here for my grandson."

"Why?" She was completely mystified. "He's only a baby. He doesn't know if you're there or not. What does it matter?"

"It matters to me. I need to be here for my daughter and her husband, too."

"But I miss you." Tina decided to try a different approach. She softened her tone and tried to be alluring. "You left so early last night, I was looking forward to being with you again today."

"Tina, don't look for me at all. I'm staying here until I know what's wrong with Nick." He had no desire to keep talking. He wanted to get off the phone and back inside the hospital. He didn't want to risk missing any news Carol might have.

"Fine," Tina answered tightly, thoroughly annoyed. She wondered at Alan's priorities. When his children had walked in on them at the office, he'd made *her* leave, not his son and daughter. And now he was choosing to sit at the hospital worrying about his grandson when he could have been spending time with her. "But don't expect me to be sitting here waiting for you."

"Fine." He hung up.

Tina hung up, too. Alan had sounded a bit stressed, but she wasn't worried. She was confident he would realize she was right—that his daughter could reach him on his cell phone wherever he was. She firmly believed he would be showing up at her place within the hour, and she would be more than ready to reward him.

After getting off the phone, Alan checked in the waiting room to see if Carol or Jim had come looking for them. They weren't there, so he decided to join Dorothy, in the chapel.

Dorothy was praying fervently when she heard the chapel door open. She glanced back to see Alan coming in. When he sat down beside her in the pew, she scooted farther over to put a definite distance between them.

They remained there for a half hour before returning to the emergency room to see if there had been any word on Nick's condition.

"Are you staying around or are you leaving?" Dorothy asked as they walked down the hall.

"I'm staying."

"But isn't your girlfriend waiting for you?"

Alan didn't know what to say, so he said nothing. She went on, "She must be very disappointed that you're not seeing her. The little black dress I sold her at my store looked stunning on her."

" 'Your' store?"

"Oh, yes. I guess I didn't tell you. I bought into Total Elegance. I'm now half-owner."

"You did what?"

"I took a whole lot of our money and bought a partnership in the boutique."

"What the hell?"

"Yes, and the dress I sold Tina was very expensive. I'm glad it cost so much. I'll take her money any day—or was it your money she was spending?" She paused to give him a knowing look. "Oh, wait, that's right—it wasn't your money. It couldn't be, because I already took all of 'your' money. She must have been spending her own."

Alan was swamped with fury. He controlled it

with an effort. "We are going to have to have a very serious talk about money real soon, Dorothy."

"Why? I'm doing fine."

"I'm not."

"You'll have to talk to my lawyer."

Tina waited expectantly for Alan to come to her. The longer she sat there biding her time, the angrier she got.

After two hours, she decided to take action of her own. She left and went to a movie, then ate out by herself. She fully expected to find a note on her door from Alan apologizing for ruining her day, and, if not a note, at least several messages on her answering machine worrying about her and telling her he missed her.

She was spitting mad when she found no note and no messages.

Alan had made no effort to contact her.

CHAPTER EIGHTEEN

"Do you need anything for the baby?" Mark asked Jenny. He wasn't ready to leave her. If he had his way, he would never be apart from her again.

"Actually, I think I have everything I need," she answered. "We just finished the nursery yesterday."

"We?"

She told him of the surprise shower. "I think Joe and Gail were behind the whole thing. They are so wonderful. Would you like to see the nursery?"

"Yes, I would."

Jenny led him upstairs to the newly decorated baby's room.

"It looks wonderful. I see you played it safe going with green paint."

"Since I don't know if it's a boy or girl, I thought I'd better stay neutral."

They both laughed.

Mark walked over to the crib as the full realization of what was about to happen hit him again. This was serious. Very soon there would be a baby sleeping here—his baby. He went back to stand before Jenny.

"Jenny, I know you don't owe me a thing, but please let me be a part of this. I want to know our child. I want to be in the baby's life—in your life."

Very tentatively he reached out and took her in his arms. It was a quiet moment. It was a moment meant for healing.

The mound of her stomach against him caused Mark to grin.

"There's more than the past coming between us," he said with a soft chuckle.

"It's our future," Jenny said.

Mark massaged her back gently to comfort her.

The feelings that stirred within her at his touch troubled Jenny, and she moved out of his embrace. "Don't. This is too fast."

"That's fine." Mark understood her reluctance as they went back downstairs. The love and intimacy they'd shared had suffered a terrible blow, but he could build on what they did have. Somehow, someday, he was going to win back her love.

He had a lot of work to do to repair the damage he'd done in his selfishness and stupidity. He was humbled now by Jenny's bravery and love for their child. He would prove to her that he was man enough to do whatever it took to provide for them and their future.

"Can I call you tomorrow?" he asked. "I could come by and bring dinner. How about I pick up your favorite pizza?" He remembered her weakness for pizza.

"I don't know . . ." Still Jenny hesitated. She felt swept away by the rush of new events. If there was one thing she'd learned from all that had happened in their relationship, it was to go slowly and not rush into anything.

"No problem. I'll give you a call." He would not push her or pressure her. He would let things develop as she wanted them to.

She walked him to the front door and saw him out. He went down the steps and out to the sidewalk before pausing to look back at her. They stared at each other across the distance for a long moment; then he lifted a hand in farewell and walked away, back toward Our Lady to get his car.

Jenny went inside and closed the door. Returning to the nursery, she stood there, taking in the beauty of the room and the promise it held.

Mark had a lot to think about on his way back to church. He caught sight of Our Lady's tall steeple with the cross on top and somehow felt stronger. He could do this. He could win back Jenny's trust and love.

It wouldn't be easy. He didn't deserve it. But he would find a way.

Nothing else mattered.

He loved her—and their child.

"Thank God," Dorothy said, immediately hugging her daughter and son-in-law.

It was after ten P.M., and they had just come to

give Dorothy and Alan the good news about the baby's condition.

"So Nick's going to be all right?" Alan asked.

"Yes. The fever has finally broken," Carol told them. "They want to keep him overnight just to be sure, but for now, everything looks okay."

Jim slipped a supportive arm around his wife. "This was scary."

"Yes, it has been," Dorothy agreed. "I'm glad they're not sending him home right away. He's just so young."

"We're glad, too," Carol said.

"Is there anything you'd like me to do?"

"If you could call David for us? I talked to him earlier and promised to let him know how Nick was doing."

"I'll call him as soon as I get home, but are you sure you don't want me to stay with you?" Dorothy deliberately did not ask if Carol wanted them both to stay.

"No. Jim's with me," Carol said. "We'll be all right, but thank you for coming, thank you for being here." She hugged her mother again, appreciative of her moral support. She'd never been through anything like this before, and she hoped it never happened again. Babies should never get sick. "You, too, Dad." She did not hug him.

"If anything changes, let me know," Dorothy said. "Otherwise, call me when you get home tomorrow."

"We will."

Jim gave his mother-in-law a quick hug and shook Alan's hand before leaving with Carol to return to their son's bedside.

"Are you ready?" Alan asked.

Dorothy was not pleased to realize she had no way to get home except with Alan. She was going to be stuck in his company even longer. "Yes. It's been a long day."

They said little on the ride to the house. Only when they pulled into the driveway did Alan speak again.

"Dorothy, we have to talk." He put the car in park and turned to face her.

"Not now, Alan." She was exhausted. Her emotions had been on a roller coaster all day. She needed some peace and quiet.

"Yes, now." He was firm. "You left me broke, Dorothy. You took all the money. Where the hell is it? I need some to live on."

"I've spent it," she answered with a cold smile. "If you have any more questions, do what I told you to do—talk to my lawyer." She opened her car door to get out. "Good-bye, Alan."

Fury filled him as he watched her enter the house and shut the door behind her.

Women! He'd had enough of all of them.

He hated them all!

He hated Tina for being so heartless. How could she expect him to just walk away from the hospital when Nick was seriously ill? It didn't matter that Nick didn't know whether he was there or not. *He* knew.

He hated Dorothy for leaving him flat-ass broke.

And, oddly, most of all, he hated Carol. First they'd had that confrontation at the office, and today she had all but ignored him at the hospital.

Alan drove away from the house in a fury. He'd already made up his mind. He was going to take advantage of the small bar in his hotel room. He needed a drink bad.

It was almost eleven o'clock. Claire had already gone to bed, but Darrell was still sitting up watching TV. Working nights messed with his sleep schedule on weekends.

A knock on the door worried him. There shouldn't be anybody coming at this time of night.

"Who is it?" he asked cautiously through the closed door, talking low so he wouldn't wake Claire.

"Who do you think it is? Open the damned door."

The all-too-familiar voice from his past gave Darrell a chill.

It was Nash.

Darrell had avoided him ever since he'd gotten out of prison. He wanted to run, but there was no place to hide.

Nash had found him.

Darrell unlocked the door and went into the hall. He found both Nash and Vince waiting for him.

"Hello, Darrell. We heard you were back." Nash and Vince were smiling at him.

"Yeah. I've been back for a while now."

"And you didn't let us know?" Nash sneered. "I'm disappointed in you."

In the past, Darrell had helped them pull off a lot of jobs. They'd been disappointed when he was arrested and convicted. Now that he was in town again, they saw no reason why they couldn't get back to business.

"Aren't you going to let us in?" Vince demanded.

"Claire's sleeping. Let's go out back."

They went into the night-shrouded backyard where Darrell hoped no one could hear them.

"What do you want? Why are you here?"

"We just came to see you, that's all. We wondered how you were doing," Nash said.

"I'm doing fine, and now that you know, you can go," Darrell said tersely, hoping they'd leave.

"You're being rude, Darrell. I expected better from you. We've missed you. We can use you again."

"You can keep right on missing me. I'm done. I ain't coming back."

"But you were so good at what you did."

"That's why I ended up in prison," Darrell countered. "Look, Nash. There's no point in talking. I'm through."

"We need you back with us," Nash insisted.

"No. I told you. I'm through. I don't want any part of it anymore."

"Shit," Vince sneered, stepping up in a threatening manner. "You're nothing but a damned coward."

Darrell didn't think there was anything the least bit cowardly about standing up to them and telling them no. He turned away in disgust.

"Don't you turn your back on us," Vince growled, ready for a fight. He wasn't averse to beating the hell out of anybody who dared to defy him.

Darrell faced the two thugs again, his rage obvious. "There's something you two need to understand. I had a lot of time to think while I was away, and I made up my mind I would never go back to prison again." He fixed his gaze on Nash. "And you know me well enough to know that when I make up my mind to do something, I do it. I got a real job now, and I'm earning a living."

"Yeah, that's why you're living so high here," Vince scoffed.

"I'm living clean, man. I don't have the cops after me. I got a good woman. I don't need you or want you around."

Nash still thought he could lure him in. "The money would be good—real good. You could take your lady and move out of this dump."

"I told you, Nash. I'm not interested. Now get the hell out of here."

Vince started toward him, fists clenched and ready for a fight, but Nash put an arm out to stop him.

"You're a fool, Darrell," Nash said coolly. "You're trying to go straight, but you don't have it in you."

"You're nothing," Vince added.

Darrell shrugged. He didn't care what these two thought of him. He just wanted them to go away and never come back. "This is the way I want it. Now go on. Get out of here. I don't want to see you around anymore."

Nash laughed eerily. "Oh, you're going to see us around. Have no doubt about that."

Darrell took a challenging step toward the two. Vince pulled a knife on him. It was a wicked-looking blade, and Darrell stopped.

"We'll be back," Nash said. "Come on, Vince."

Vince was cursing Darrell as he put his knife away. The two thugs walked off and disappeared into the night.

Darrell returned to the apartment and locked the door securely. Even as he did it, though, he knew that a simple deadbolt could not keep him safe.

He wondered miserably if anything could keep him safe from his past.

Tina was thoroughly disgusted. She lay in her solitary bed staring at the sexy black dress hanging in her closet. She had spent a lot on that dress and had thought she would get her money's worth out of it. She had expected Alan to have second thoughts about his decision to stay at the hospital. She had thought he would change his mind and show up. As each hour had passed and Alan still hadn't come, Tina had grown more and more fed up.

The first chance she got, she was going to confront him and force him to make a decision. When he'd left his wife, she'd believed he was serious about pursuing a new relationship, but his choosing his family over her today had been a true slap in the face. She wasn't used to being treated this way.

There were other men who could fill Alan's place in her life—and her bed.

She wondered if she should start looking around when she got to work in the morning.

Tina smiled at the thought of a new conquest.

CHAPTER NINETEEN
DAY SEVEN

The Lord Has Done Great Things for Us . . .

Dorothy was eager to go to church the following morning. She had a lot to be thankful for today. She hadn't heard anything new from Carol overnight, so Nick had to be doing all right. He would be home today, and she would stop by and see him.

As she drove to Our Lady, Dorothy thought of Alan. She smiled to herself. Never in all their years of marriage had she stood up to him the way she had last night. She had always tried to please him, to make sure his life was perfect, but no more. She was proud of herself. She was stronger now and she was going to take care of Dorothy first. It wasn't selfishness. It was survival.

She would start the day with church and then concentrate all her efforts on trying to make Total Elegance *the* place to shop in town. She had several great ideas to share with Paige when she got to work.

It was going to be a wonderful day.

She was sure of it.

Alan woke with a headache, and he knew he deserved it. He'd helped himself to the minibar in his room and had finally fallen asleep long after midnight. Morning had come far too early for his taste, but there was no avoiding it. It was Monday. He had to go to work.

His mood was no less surly as he showered and shaved. For the first time in as long as he could remember, he did not want to go to the office. He didn't want to see anyone at Warson-Freeman. He particularly didn't want to see Tina. He just wanted to be left alone.

Just a few days ago, Alan could have taken time off, but not anymore. He had to work. He had no money in the bank to cover his expenses. He was back to living as he had when he'd first started working full-time after graduating from college some thirty-five years ago. It had been a payday-to-payday existence. It hadn't been easy then, and it wasn't going to be easy now—especially since he'd become accustomed to a certain lifestyle at home.

Home—

Alan admitted to himself for the first time that he missed his home. His lawyer had told him that, since he was the one who'd walked out on the marriage, the divorce wasn't going to be easy or pretty. Dorothy held the moral high ground.

She had let him know it, too, at the hospital yesterday. Dorothy had never acted this way before. The change in her was startling. He wondered what had happened to the woman he'd married.

He told himself he didn't care.

He didn't care about anything.

Alan's mood was dark about his whole life in general, but he did have one thing to be happy about. His grandson was going to be all right. Nick was going to be fine.

Claire was surprised when Darrell got up early with her the next morning and started getting dressed.

"Why are you up and moving at the crack of dawn? This is your day to sleep late."

"I thought I'd go to six-thirty."

She understood. "If I had time, I'd go with you."

"I know. I'll see you after work."

"Yes, you will," she said with certainty, giving him a kiss as he left their apartment.

Darrell made it to Our Lady earlier than usual. He was glad. He wanted some quiet time to pray before Mass began. The unexpected visit from Nash and Vince worried him deeply. They meant nothing but trouble. They always had been trouble, and they always would be. He didn't want anything to do with them. He hoped they would stay away, but he had his doubts.

Darrell saw Jenny come in, and they smiled in greeting to each other. Others entered, too, and finally Father Walters made his way up the center aisle to the altar.

"The grace and peace of God our Father and the Lord Jesus Christ be with you," he intoned.

Darrell was attentive, listening to the readings and the Gospel. He was glad Father Walters had Mass this morning. He wanted to talk with him again. This time as the parishioners filed forward for Communion, Darrell did not leave. He stayed in his pew, waiting.

When Mass ended and the priest left the altar to greet people in the foyer, Darrell sought him out.

"It's good to see you again," Father Walters said as he shook Darrell's hand. "How are you?"

"I need to talk to you again."

"Of course." Father Walters didn't hesitate to usher Darrell into the private office and shut the door. "Please, sit down. I've been worrying about you—and praying for you."

"Thanks." Darrell was a little embarrassed, but he was very aware he needed all the prayers he could get.

"How are things going?"

"I did what you suggested. I told Claire what had happened. We went to the police."

"Good. Have they caught the gunman yet?"

"No."

Father looked grim. "How are you holding up? Are you doing all right?"

"I wish I could tell you yes, but I'd be lying." Darrell shook his head. "Some of my old friends found me last night at home. They want me back working with them. I told them I didn't want anything to do with them."

"I'm proud of you." Father Walters was amazed by Darrell's strength of character. A lot of ex-cons fell right back into their old, dangerous ways. He was glad Darrell was smarter than that.

Darrell hadn't realized how much the holy man's praise would mean to him. "I just hope they stay away from me."

"I'll pray on that for you."

"Father Walters—" Darrell looked up at him, unsure.

The priest had no idea what was troubling the other man.

"I need to talk to you about one other thing."

"Yes?" The priest worried that something else had gone terribly wrong in Darrell's life. It always amazed him how some people could go through life with very little strife and misery, while others seemed dogged by trouble.

"I think it's time . . . I've been thinking about this for a while . . ."

"What?"

"I want to convert."

Father Walters had been hoping and praying for guidance for Darrell. He was delighted at this revelation. "The Holy Spirit is definitely with you."

"You think so, huh?"

"I know so. Do you know how much courage it took for you to realize what you needed in your life? Fortitude is one of the gifts of the Holy Spirit. You'll learn all about that in R.C.I.A."

"What's that?"

"It's the Rite of Christian Initiation of Adults. It's a course you have to take to learn about the church and our religion. Once you complete the course, you'll be confirmed at the Easter Vigil. Have you ever been baptized?"

"No."

Father Walters nodded. "We can baptize you at the Vigil, too."

"I'd like that. When does that R.C.I.A. program start?"

"It's already started, but you can still join us. We meet on Tuesday nights at seven."

Darrell was disappointed. "I work nights. There's no way I can get a weeknight off."

Father Walters looked thoughtful. "If you're really serious about this, I can work with you personally."

"You'd do that?" Darrell was surprised by his generous offer.

"Yes. Wait here a minute," he said, standing up. "I'll get you one of the books, and you can get started reading on your own. Then we can meet one morning a week after six-thirty Mass and go over the material. How does that work for you?"

"That would be great. Thanks, Father."

"I'll be right back."

A short time later, Darrell left Our Lady, book in hand. Father Walters definitely was bringing Jesus to people—the way he'd talked to him that first morning when he was sneaking through the walkway, and now offering to help him join the church. Darrell made up his mind not to disappoint him. He was going through with this. He would talk to Claire about it, too, and see if she was interested in taking instructions.

Quickening his pace, Darrell hurried toward home. He was hoping to catch Claire before she left for work, and he was eager to get started reading.

Jenny lingered in her pew to offer up more thanks to God for all the wonderful things that had happened in her life—her friends, the shower, Mark showing up so unexpectedly. She knew now, without a doubt, that she had made the right decision to keep her baby. She smiled as she thought of the pacifier in her purse. Ever since she'd found it that day at the hospital, she'd kept it with her. Once the baby came, she was going to put it in a place of honor in the nursery. That way, not a day would go by when she would not remember everything that had happened. After saying one last "thank you," Jenny got up and left the church. It was time to go to work.

"Good morning, little girl," Joe said, grinning mischievously. He had lingered out in the parking lot in the hope of getting a chance to talk to her.

"Yes, it is a good morning." Jenny went straight to him and gave him a hug.

"How's everything going? Are you feeling well today?"

"I am feeling fantastic. I have to tell you, this was one exciting weekend. First you gave me the shower, and then—"

"Did something else happen?" His hopes soared that Mark Seton might have acted on his message.

"Yes! Mark came to see me. In fact, he was waiting for me after church yesterday morning."

Joe couldn't believe he'd missed him, but he was thrilled Mark had taken action. "After all this time, he showed up." He sounded thoughtful. "That's amazing. I take it you talked with him. How did it go?"

"Oh, yes, we talked. He had no idea I was still pregnant, so he was shocked."

"What did he say?"

"He said he loved me." She looked at Joe, her expression more serious. "I had trouble believing him after all that's happened."

"I understand. Just seeing him again had to be upsetting for you."

"Upsetting—and wonderful." Her gaze met his. "Is it wrong for me to still care about him?"

He understood her confusion and wanted to help. "Just the fact that Mark came to you after all these months is amazing. Maybe God is at work here. Maybe God has a plan. Your Mark sounds like he's basically a good man."

"I always believed he was . . . before."

"Can you give him another chance?"

"I'm scared," she admitted openly. "I'm afraid to trust him again. He hurt me so badly—"

"I know how you feel, but it sounds like Mark has changed."

"I think he has. I hope he has."

"Then remember what Jesus said: 'We must forgive seventy times seven.'"

"That's the problem." Jenny realized her fear. "I have to forgive him if we're going to make it work between us."

"It won't be easy. Nobody ever said forgiving was easy. You've been hurt, badly, but it sounds like he's truly sorry and honestly wants to make it up to you."

"I think he does," she said.

"Then you've got nothing to lose and everything to gain. He is the father of your child. You'll always be connected to him that way, no matter what you decide. Do you love him?"

Jenny looked up at Joe, a bit shamefaced to admit it openly. "Yes. I still do."

"Then don't waste this opportunity for happiness."

"Oh, Joe, what would I do without you?" She hugged him again, glad for his sage advice.

"I hope we never have to find out," he laughed, enjoying her embrace.

"I have to go to work. It's getting late."

"Have a good day. Will I see you in the morning?"

"Absolutely."

Joe waited and watched Jenny drive away. He was smiling as he walked to his car. He couldn't wait to get to work so he could call Gail and tell her the good news.

Mark got up early and called his mother at home. He was surprised when he got no answer, but he figured she'd probably gone into work super-early this morning to get caught up after being away for a week. Mark would have preferred to talk to her about Jenny in private somewhere away from the office, but it looked like that wasn't going to happen.

As prepared as he would ever be to face her, Mark headed for work. He reached his office so early, Joanne wasn't even there yet, and she always beat him to work.

Mark took advantage of the few minutes alone. Since he was going to be facing his mother with the news about Jenny and their child, he had to plan exactly how he was going to handle things. It was reasonable to assume their conversation wouldn't go smoothly. Mark knew exactly how his mother felt about Jenny.

Grimacing inwardly, he sat down at his desk. He no longer cared what his mother wanted or what was best for Seton Leasing. He had put the company first for years, but no more.

In the time he and Jenny had been apart, he'd been miserable. Jenny and their child were now the most important part of his life. He was going to do whatever was necessary to provide for them—with or without the benefit of marriage.

Mark knew he was being ridiculous even to think she would simply fall back into his arms after what had happened between them. He had a lot of making up to do. He would have to prove the seriousness of his intentions. Jenny had every reason in the world to doubt him.

Picking up the phone, Mark dialed his mother's extension and waited. He was surprised when she didn't answer. He'd expected her to be at her desk hard at work.

"What are you doing here?" Joanne asked, standing in his doorway. "I thought you'd be late getting in today after your big weekend in the country."

"No. I've got too much to do this morning."

"You ready for coffee?"

"Absolutely. I'm going to need all the energy I can get today."

She hurried off to get his much-needed dose of caffeine.

Mark glanced at the clock.

His mother would be arriving at Seton Leasing at any moment.

He was ready.

CHAPTER TWENTY

Margo was smiling as she parked in her priority reserved spot in the Seton Leasing garage. Mark's car was parked in his space, so she knew he was already at his desk. She was glad, for she was anxious to see him and find out how his weekend with the Barretts had gone. The prospect of a family "merger" with the Barretts was almost too good to be true. *Mark and Christine Seton*—yes, she liked the sound of that very much.

Margo went straight to her office on the top floor to drop off her briefcase, then hurried to find Mark.

"Good morning, Joanne. I take it my son's already here?"

"Yes, ma'am. Bright and early," Joanne responded. "Would you like some coffee? I just brought Mark his."

"Yes, thanks."

Margo walked into Mark's office without knocking.

"How did it go? How was your weekend?" she asked without preamble.

Mark looked up from his desk. "It was one fantastic weekend."

She beamed at the news as she sat down in one of the chairs opposite his desk. "Tell me all about it. I bet the Barretts' lodge is magnificent." She was eager to hear all the details. Their short conversation Saturday had hardly been enough to satisfy her.

"The lodge was very nice, but that isn't what was so great."

"Then, what?" Margo waited. She expected to hear wonderful things about Christine.

"Well, I have something to tell you, and as happy as I am about it, I don't think you're going to feel the same way."

"What are you talking about?" Margo was puzzled. If the weekend had been so magnificent, what could possibly be wrong?

Mark looked her straight in the eye. "Congratulations. You're going to be a grandmother."

Immediately, Margo assumed he was talking about Christine being pregnant. "How could you think I wouldn't be happy? This is fantastic news. I had no idea you and Christine had been that close, but it doesn't matter."

Somehow Mark had known she would jump to the wrong conclusion. "Mom—"

"What matters is, we start planning your wedding right now!" She was ignoring him as she started making arrangements in her mind.

"Mom!" He stood up to assert himself.

"And we'll have to—"

"*Mom!*" Mark was almost shouting as Joanne appeared in the doorway with Margo's coffee. He looked at Joanne and waved her out, ordering, "Not now, and close the door."

Joanne didn't hesitate. She recognized that no-nonsense tone; Mark only used it in the most serious situations.

"Mark—" Margo said his name in great irritation, "I wanted my coffee."

"Later," he said tersely.

Margo was shocked.

"Mark, I said—" she began in her most authoritative tone.

"Mother," he ground out, cutting her off. "It's not Christine I'm talking about."

Mark finally had her full and undivided attention.

"What!" She stared at him in confusion.

"It's Jenny."

Now Margo was truly perplexed. "Jenny? But we took care of it."

"No, 'we' didn't take care of 'it,' but Jenny has. Jenny has taken care of everything—all by herself for all these months. She was the smart one. She realized she was carrying our son or daughter, and she refused to kill our child just because it was an inconvenience."

"This is unacceptable," Margo stated hotly.

"It's happening, so accept it," Mark dictated, striding around his desk to stand before her. "I love Jenny, and I love the child she's carrying—my child. I fully intend to be a part of their lives. In fact, I'm going to propose to Jenny, but I won't be surprised if she turns me down."

"You can't marry her!"

"Oh, yes, I can," he said firmly. "If she turns me down the first time, I'll keep trying. I won't give up. If I have to beg her to marry me, I will. She means that much to me."

"But you have to marry someone like Christine—someone who's wealthy and socially connected!"

"No. I don't," Mark stated just as categorically.

She saw how determined he seemed and decided to force his hand. "What about the company? If you marry her, I'll—"

"You'll what?" he challenged. "Fire me? Go ahead. I'll get another job. I love Jenny, and I intend to spend the rest of my life proving that to her."

"You're a fool." Margo's shock was complete.

"Yes, I am. I'm a fool in love," Mark said. "I've been miserable all these months Jenny and I have been apart. I don't know what I was thinking—leaving her the way I did." He thought of Jenny facing her pregnancy alone. "I tried to lose myself in my work. I tried to keep busy so I wouldn't realize what I was missing, but I could never forget her. Without Jenny, I only existed. I love her. She means everything to me. You loved Dad, didn't you?" When his mother didn't answer right away, he asked again, "Didn't you?"

Still she didn't answer.

"If that's the way it's going to be with you, then I'm out of here. I'm happy now. If you're not, I'm sorry for you." Mark started to walk out of the office. "I need to go shopping. I need to buy a ball glove and a bat, or maybe I should get a Barbie doll—"

With that, he quit the office, leaving his mother staring after him.

"Joanne, I'll be out the rest of the day."

Mark didn't pause as he strode past his secretary's desk and kept going.

He had to go to the toy store to buy a present or two or three.

He was smiling.

Joanne watched him leave in amazement. She had overheard the conversation through the closed door, and she was proud of Mark. She had always known he was a fine man, and he'd just proven it. She wondered if his mother realized it.

Margo sat alone in the office, unmoving. She wasn't certain what had just happened. She had come to see Mark this morning to hear about his time with Christine and her family. She had never expected anything like this. She had thought Jenny was out of his life forever. Obviously, she'd been wrong.

"Mrs. Seton? Can I get you anything?" Joanne asked from the open doorway. "Would you like your coffee now?"

"No." Margo stood and walked past without saying another word.

You loved Dad, didn't you?

Mark's words echoed within her.

Margo thought of Grant, her long-dead husband, and her heart ached. Yes, she had loved Grant more than anything in the whole world, and when he'd died at such a young age, it had been traumatic for her. She'd feared she would never recover from the loss. Only her work and her love for their son had saved her.

You loved Dad, didn't you?

She thought of Mark and the way he'd acted this morning. She'd always known he was a serious negotiator and businessman, but she'd never seen him this way. He'd reminded her of his father—powerful and determined, going after what he wanted. Determined to reach his goal no matter what stood in his way.

Mark had just shown her that he was willing to give up everything for love.

Painfully, she understood.

Years ago, she would have done no less to be with Grant.

Tina waited all morning for Alan's call. She'd thought he would contact her first thing. As the hours passed and she heard nothing, her irritation with him turned to worry. It didn't suit her to go looking for him right away, but she found she was growing a bit concerned.

By the time the noon hour arrived, Tina had

made up her mind what to do. She headed straight for Alan's office. She hoped to catch him alone while his secretary was out to lunch. The thought of what she could do to him there made her smile. She wanted to get his thoughts back solely on her.

"Hello, Miss Lawrence," Alan's secretary greeted her. "What can I do for you?"

Tina was piqued to see her. "I wanted to speak with Alan for a moment." She expected to be shown right in.

"I'm sorry, but he's gone."

"Gone? Where?"

"He had family business to take care of. Can I take a message or have him call you?"

"No. I'll catch up with him later. Thanks."

Tina kept her pleasant expression plastered on her face until she was alone in the elevator returning to her office. Only then did she let her fury show.

Family business?

Alan had ignored her completely yesterday because of his family, and now again today.

Her rage gnawed at her.

Alan had left his wife for her.

Didn't that mean she was supposed to come first in his life?

Tina had wanted to marry him. That had been her grandiose plan from the first moment she'd set her sights on him. She'd expected to be first in his life.

She now saw far too clearly where she ranked in importance to Alan, and she didn't like it one bit.

She would not play second fiddle to anyone. The man she married would have to build his world around her. She refused to be treated like her mother. She had too much pride to let any man ever treat her badly. If Alan was always going to be at the beck and call of his children and grandchildren, then she was going to have to rethink their relationship, and she didn't see much of a future for them.

There were other men who would suit her purposes, men with money and power.

Her career came first.

She was going to start looking around.

The prospect didn't trouble her at all.

Mark hadn't been in a toy store for ages, and it showed. He wandered up and down the aisles, amazed by what he saw. He was glad to find that there were still Transformers and Star Wars toys, and of course there were Barbies, but he didn't linger long in that aisle.

He didn't feel too old if toy stores were still selling Transformers. He had quite a collection stashed away at home. He hadn't looked at them in years, but seeing them on the shelves here made him miss them. He decided to dig them out the first chance he got.

Mark went through the infant toys and picked out a stuffed dog with a music box in it. He'd always wanted a dog when he was growing up, but his mother would never allow it. She hated dogs.

Stuffed dog under his arm, Mark found the

bats and balls and gloves and bought all the equipment suitable for the youngest child. That done, he braved the girls' stuff again and bought a baby doll, just in case.

Mark wasn't averse to having a daughter. He just wasn't quite sure what to do with one. It would definitely be a learning experience for him.

After checking out, Mark was walking through the mall to the parking lot when a jewelry store caught his eye. A glimmer of an idea came to him.

"Why not?" he muttered to himself.

He went straight there to look at engagement rings. With only one quick glance in the lighted case, a heart-shaped diamond ring caught his eye.

"Can I help you, sir?" a salesman asked.

"I want that engagement ring. I need a size seven."

"Let me check for you." He took the set out and said, "This is a seven."

"I'll take it."

It was the easiest sale the man had ever made.

Mark didn't question his good fortune in finding a ring that just happened to be the right size for Jenny. He didn't know how long it would take him to convince her to marry him, but he didn't intend to give up.

Mark made his plan for the evening. He would call Jenny and arrange for them to eat in. He would bring her favorite pizza; and put the ring in the pizza box.

It was worth a try.

The worst she could say would be "no," and

then he'd have to come up with another idea for winning her heart.

He was determined.

One way or another, she was going to be Mrs. Mark Seton.

"Dad—what are you doing here?" Carol was shocked to see her father standing there when she answered the door. He never left work early— never.

"I was worrying about Nick and wanted to come by and see him. I take it he's all better, since you are here." Alan entered the house and followed his daughter into the family room, where they sat down to talk.

"He's doing fine. He's sleeping now. The pediatrician said he was looking much better this morning. His fever has broken."

"Thank heaven."

"Exactly. The doctor seemed confident he was going to be all right. He said it might take him a day or two to bounce back to normal."

"What a relief."

"It was scary, that's for sure. Thank you for coming to the hospital. I really appreciated your being there. I know it couldn't have been easy for you with Mom being there, too."

"We had to be there. Nick is our grandson. We love him."

"Dad—" Carol was trying to find the right words to have a frank discussion with him about his plans for the future. "What are you doing?"

"What do you mean?"

She gathered her courage. "You know what I mean—leaving Mom to run around with that . . . that slut. How could you, after all you and Mom have meant to each other? Do you really love this Tina? Is that why you did this?"

Alan was caught off guard by her directness. He hadn't talked with anyone about Tina, and he wasn't about to start now, especially not with his own daughter.

"It's none of your business, Carol." He tried not to sound arrogant.

"This woman destroys my family and it's none of my business?"

"There comes a time in a man's life—"

"—when some slut comes on to you and you leave your wife and family behind for a piece of ass?" she interrupted him. Carol knew she was being crude, but she didn't care. Her father was so enamored with that Tina, she knew it would take something blunt to get through to him. "You're obviously not thinking with your brain anymore."

Alan stood up to leave. "I'll talk to you later. Kiss Nick for me."

He walked out without another word.

Carol stood in her doorway and watched him drive away. For a moment, she regretted trying to get him to talk about his affair, but then she quit worrying about it. She'd always thought her father was an intelligent man. She hoped that was still true. If it was, she believed that eventually he would realize the error of his ways and come around.

Carol realized the problem was that she wasn't sure whether her mother would still care when he did.

Alan looked at the clock in his car. It was only midafternoon. He knew he could return to work, but decided against it. His life was a mess and he needed some time alone to think. He thought about returning to his hotel room, but as he looked up, he saw the steeple of Our Lady.

The church was always open.

Taking care of sinners wasn't a 9 to 5 job.

It was 24/7/365.

Alan turned his car in that direction.

CHAPTER TWENTY-ONE

"All right," Jenny told Mark over the phone. "I'll see you a little after six."

She was smiling as she hung up. She pivoted her desk chair to find Donna standing in her office doorway, watching her.

"Have you got a hot date tonight?" Donna asked, curious. She hadn't seen Jenny this happy in ages, and wondered who she was going to be seeing.

"I am so glad you're here. There's so much I have to tell you!"

"I got your message earlier, but I've been in meetings all morning. What is it? What happened?" Donna knew the news had to be good.

Jenny quickly explained everything about Mark's reappearance in her life.

"Your prayers really were answered. This is so wonderful!" Donna went to give her a big hug.

"But, Donna . . ." Jenny began.

"What?" She heard the uncertainty in her friend's voice.

"I'm scared."

"I don't blame you. I'd be scared, too, if I'd been through everything you've been through. But you said he apologized."

"Yes, he did." Jenny looked up at her hopefully. "He even told me he would quit his job if that was what it took to prove how serious he was about wanting to be back in my life."

"What are you going to do?"

"Well, for starters, I'm going to have pizza for dinner tonight." Jenny chuckled. "Mark's coming over around six o'clock."

"That's a fine way to start. Pizza."

"Yes, it is. The only thing better is ice cream."

"See if you can get him to take you out to Dairy Queen afterward."

"That's not a bad idea." Jenny was smiling, then slowly got serious again. "Donna, I hope I'm doing the right thing."

"You are. Trust your instincts. I know you believe you still love him, but you've come this far on your own. You've proven you can make it. You're a strong woman, Jenny. You'll make the right decision about what's the best thing for you and your baby."

"You're right." She was always glad for Donna's calming advice. "I can handle this. Everything really is going to be all right."

"Enjoy your pizza! I've got to get back to work."

"I'll talk to you tomorrow."

"I'll be waiting to hear from you."

Mark was excited, and he didn't get excited very often anymore. With his backseat full of toys, a large pizza on the front passenger seat and the diamond engagement ring safely stowed in its box in his pocket, he was as ready as he would ever be to propose to Jenny. He'd tried to think of a more romantic way to ask her to marry him, but putting the ring in the box with the pizza still seemed the best way to get the answer he wanted. If it took promising to buy her pizza every night of the week for the rest of their lives, he would do it. He just wanted to be eating those pizzas with her and their child.

Mark parked in front of Jenny's house. He couldn't carry everything at once, so he took the toys first. He was feeling a little nervous as he rang the doorbell and waited for her to let him in.

Jenny was still finding it hard to believe that Mark was really there on her porch, ringing her doorbell. It was true. Everything that had happened hadn't been a dream.

"You're here," she said with a slightly uncertain smile as she opened the door.

"Yes, I am, and I've brought some important things with me," he said, lifting the bag so she could see the toy store's name on it.

"You went toy shopping?" Jenny was amazed.

"That's right, and it was quite an experience. Wait until you see all the cool stuff I bought." He put the bag on her sofa. "I left the pizza out in the car. I'll be right back."

He hurried out to the car again. Once he was sure Jenny wasn't watching him, he slipped the ring box into a corner of the pizza box. On the way back to the house, he actually found himself saying a silent prayer that she would accept his proposal.

While Mark had gone to get the food, Jenny couldn't resist peeking in the bag of toys. She fell in love at first sight with the stuffed dog and pulled it out to cuddle it.

"Mark, this is so cute!" she told him, looking up as he let himself in the house.

"You like dogs?"

"I love dogs."

"Well, this one is special. It plays music, too. Wind it up."

Jenny did, and listened in delight to the sweet rendition of "How Much Is That Doggy in the Window?"

"I don't know." she said thoughtfully, hugging it close. "I may keep this one for myself."

"So you're going to teach our baby about sharing toys right away, are you?" he teased.

"That's right." Jenny grinned.

"Where do you want to eat? Here or the kitchen?"

"Let's eat in the kitchen. We'll have more room."

Still carrying the stuffed dog, Jenny led the way to the kitchen table. Mark trailed after her and put the pizza box in the middle of the table.

"You sit down and rest," he told her. "I'll take care of everything."

"Now, this is what I call service. You not only brought the dinner, but you're waiting on tables, too." Jenny was laughing. "Are animals allowed at this establishment?"

"Absolutely. Do you want to use plates?"

"No, we can eat out of the box. Why dirty the dishes?"

"Exactly. What do you want to drink?"

"Water is fine for me. There's some soda in the fridge. Help yourself."

Mark brought Jenny a glass of water and got himself a soda. He grabbed a few napkins and settled in across the table from her.

"All right, dig in," he encouraged.

Mark was a confident man. He could wheel and deal with the best of them. He could face down corporate execs and not blink an eye, but he found he was actually nervous as he sat there waiting for her to open the box.

Jenny was hungry. There was no doubt about that. She put the stuffed dog on the table next to her and reached out to lift the lid, ready for some sustenance.

Jenny's breath caught in her throat.

She was unable to believe her eyes.

The pepperoni and sausage pizza looked delicious, but the ring box nestled in the corner of the box stunned her.

She looked up at Mark.

"Mark?"

He got up and went to her side. Picking up the jewelry box, he opened it and took out the engagement ring. He knelt down. "Jenny Emerson, will you marry me?"

Jenny had expected to love every bite of her dinner, but she had never expected anything like this. She turned to him. "I always knew there was a reason I loved pizza."

"Marry me, Jenny. I love you."

"Oh, Mark—" Jenny stared at the ring he was holding out to her, then lifted her gaze to his.

"If you marry me, we can have pizza for dinner as often as you like," Mark told her.

"You promise?" she asked, trying not to smile.

"I promise."

With that, the tension within her broke. She laughed out loud and threw her arms around his neck. "What girl could turn down a proposal like that?"

"You'll marry me?" Mark held her back from him so he could look in her face.

"Yes, Mark. I'll marry you."

The emotions that swept through him were powerful as he stared at her. Without saying another word, he took her hand and slipped the ring onto her finger. The ring fit perfectly, just as he'd hoped.

Jenny stared down at the heart-shaped diamond on her hand.

"It's beautiful." She looked at him, finally letting go of all her uncertainty. "We can do this. We can make this work."

"Yes, we can." There was no doubt in Mark's mind, either. They were meant to be together.

"Kiss me," Jenny said in a whisper.

Mark responded gently, leaning forward to capture her lips in a cherishing caress—a kiss of pure devotion and love.

The kiss ended, and they slowly drew apart. Jenny looked up at him and saw the depth of emotion mirrored in his eyes. Her heart ached with the knowledge of what they had almost lost. When she lifted one hand to touch his cheek, he captured her hand in his own and pressed a kiss to her palm.

"Do you want to elope tonight? I don't know where we could go, but we could probably find somebody to marry us around here. Hey, I know! We could fly to Reno or Vegas. There's probably still a flight out later tonight. What do you say?" Mark wasn't the least bit worried about missing work. He was only concerned with making Jenny his wife before their baby was born.

Jenny was smiling at him. "I don't want to go to Reno or Vegas. I want to be married here—at Our Lady."

"You do?" Mark frowned.

"Yes. We can go to the church tonight and see if Father Walters is there. He'll be able to tell us what we need to do to get married in church."

"Is there time? I want to be married before the baby is born."

"I'm sure there's some way we can do it."

Mark leaned toward her and kissed her again, then stood up. "Now the big question is . . ."

"What?" Jenny looked up at him expectantly.

"Do we eat our pizza first or go to the church?"

Jenny didn't hesitate. "We eat."

They were both laughing as they settled in to enjoy their dinner.

"You know, I think this is the best pizza I've ever had," Jenny told him, savoring a big bite.

"Me, too."

Alan didn't know what he had expected to happen at church, but whatever it was, he'd been disappointed. He'd stayed there in a back pew for a long time, praying and meditating. He had sought answers and inner peace. They had both eluded him. Frustrated, he'd left Our Lady, picked up some fast food and gone back to the hotel.

Once he'd finished eating, Alan decided he needed to go see Tina and let her know what had happened that day. He was certain she wasn't very happy with him right now, but he figured he could make it up to her. He was sure she would get over it. He headed for her apartment.

* * *

Tina answered her doorbell and smiled warmly up at Brian McCall.

"I was hoping it was you," she purred.

"I told you I'd be here at seven," Brian said with an easy grin. "I'm a man of my word."

"I like that about you." She stood back to let him in. "Give me a minute to get my purse and I'll be ready to go."

"Did you want to have dinner or just go to the club?"

"Let's go to the club. I've heard that the band playing there tonight is a good one, and I'm in the mood for some fun."

Tina cast one quick glance in the mirror in her bedroom as she grabbed up her purse. Yes, the little black dress looked good on her. It was one of her best investments, and she intended to get her money's worth out of it tonight with Brian. He was on his way to becoming a vice-president in personnel at Warson-Freeman. She couldn't imagine a better step up on her ladder to the top.

"I'm ready." She came to stand before him, smiling brightly.

"You look wonderful."

"Thanks. Let's go. We're going to have fun tonight."

As they left Tina's apartment, she walked a bit ahead of him down the hall, and Brian admired the view. His instincts told him she was one hot woman, and he was eager to find out. He'd heard rumors that she was seeing Alan Pennington from the Engineering Division, but he found it hard to believe she would waste her time on him. Pennington was far too old for Tina, plus he was married. Brian planned to prove that he could be a lot more exciting. She was relatively new in town, so he was going to take her for a walk on the wild side.

They rode the elevator down to the lobby making small talk.

"I'll go get the car from the garage and pick you up out front. How's that?" Brian offered.

"Fine."

He disappeared out the door, leaving Tina waiting in the lobby. As she walked toward the door to keep watch for Brian, she stopped. There, coming through the door, was none other than Alan.

"Tina—there you are," he greeted her. He was surprised to find her downstairs.

"I'm just on my way out, Alan," she said indifferently.

"But I came here to see you," he protested.

"I told you I wouldn't wait for you, and I'm a woman who means what she says." At that moment, she caught sight of Brian pulling up in his Porsche and started to walk past Alan.

He took her arm, stopping her. "Tina, I gave up my life for you—"

"Please," she drawled sarcastically. "You didn't give anything up for me. You did exactly what you wanted to do, and that's what I'm doing now. Good-bye, Alan."

She pulled free of his hold on her arm and walked out, leaving him behind.

Alan turned and watched as she climbed into the sports car with a younger man who looked familiar. He was certain he had seen him before—possibly at work.

Tina buckled her seat belt as Brian sped off.

"Who was that you were talking to?" he asked. He thought the man had looked like Pennington, but he hadn't been able to tell for sure.

"No one. No one at all," Tina answered lightly, and she found she truly meant it.

Tina turned her brightest smile and full attention on Brian as she rested one hand lightly on his thigh. Yes, she decided, she was definitely going to enjoy the night to come.

Stan Schmidt was about to leave his office. It was late. He was tired and more than ready to go home and try to relax. He had just reached the door when his phone rang again. He wanted to keep going, to pretend he hadn't heard the phone, but in his job, he knew he couldn't afford to ignore any call. It might be a desperate call for help, and he had to be available.

"Hello?"

"Is this Stan Schmidt?"

"Yes, it is."

"This is Officer Anderson at police headquarters. I wanted to let you know we found the car identified by Darrell Miller. The plates on it were stolen."

"Did you get any fingerprints?" Stan was hopeful.

"No. The car was burned."

"So there's nothing left to help you find the shooter?"

"No, nothing, but we aren't about to give up," Anderson answered. "Tell your man that if he thinks of anything else significant to let us know. Right now, we're back to square one, and we need all the help we can get."

"I'll relay your message."

"Thanks. I'll be in touch if I hear anything new."

Stan hung up the phone, troubled by the news. He had been hoping that the murderer would be quickly found after Darrell had given the police the information on the vehicle, but it wasn't going to happen.

He glanced at the clock and decided to try to catch Darrell at home to give him the news. He got a busy signal, so he took Darrell's home number and work number with him. He would call him again once he got home. It was important that Darrell heard the news as soon as possible.

CHAPTER TWENTY-TWO

Father Walters faced Jenny and Mark across the table in the private meeting room. He had listened to their request and was ready to answer them, although he was certain it wasn't the answer they wanted to hear.

"We need about six months to properly prepare," he told them.

"No—we want to get married right away," Mark objected.

"I understand why you're in a hurry, but you need to understand what a serious commitment marriage is."

"We understand, Father," Jenny said earnestly.

"Good, then you'll also understand why it's so important for you to go through the Marriage Preparation Program."

"Why can't you just marry us now before the

253

baby comes?" Mark was surprised that something couldn't be done.

"Because your marriage shouldn't be about the baby. Your marriage and your baby are two different issues. Why have you waited so long to think about marrying?" he challenged.

"We've been apart, and just realized we were supposed to be together," Mark admitted, embarrassed.

"So there are problems in your relationship that need to be addressed?"

"Not anymore," Jenny put in, hoping she could change Father Walters's mind. "We've worked everything out."

"How long have you been back together?" he asked perceptively.

"A few days." She had to tell the truth.

Father Walters did not waiver. "It doesn't really affect your child, whether you're married or not when he's born. He'll have a mother and a father. You will both be in his life. Wouldn't it be better if he had parents who were willing to work to stay together in their marriage?"

Jenny understood what he was saying, but was disappointed by his counsel. Everything else had worked out so wonderfully, she had thought getting married to Mark would, too.

"Marriage is a lifetime commitment two people make to one another," Father went on, "not something you rush into or feel forced into."

"What do we need to do?" Mark asked. His euphoria had passed. He was ready to get serious.

Father Walters took the time to explain the entire marriage preparation process to them.

"Sign us up," Jenny told him. "The sooner we get started, the better."

He took down their information.

"I'll call you with the meeting dates," he promised as he showed them out.

Mark walked in silence with Jenny to the car. He opened the door for her and helped her in, then went around to the driver's side.

"You're awfully quiet," Jenny said, wondering at his feelings over the matter.

"I'm disappointed, that's all," he said as he slid into the driver's seat. "I wanted us to be married before the baby was born."

"I was hoping we could be, too, but Father Walters is right. We have to be serious about this."

Mark looked over at her. "I am serious, Jenny. More serious than I've ever been in my life."

With that, he leaned over, wanting to kiss her.

Jenny started to giggle because, as big as she was, the console was in her way. "I never had this problem with your console before."

He chuckled, too, and turned back to start the car.

They were quiet as they drove to Jenny's home.

"My offer still stands," Mark finally said. "We can fly out to Vegas this weekend and get married in a civil ceremony, if you want."

"I'm in no condition to fly anywhere."

"Do you want to go to a justice of the peace

here in town? We could get our license tomorrow and marry on Saturday at the courthouse."

"I'm not sure what to do," she admitted.

When Mark pulled up in front of her house, he turned to her. His mood was solemn. "Jenny, you know that no matter when we make it legal, I won't ever leave you again. I love you, and I intend to be with you and our child always."

"Thank you, Mark."

"There's no reason for you to thank me. I should never have let us be separated in the first place. I'm proud of the decision you made to have the baby. You are such a strong, brave woman."

"You really think so?" She was surprised by his compliment.

"I know so. There aren't many women who could do what you've done. You've shown me the importance of standing up for what you believe in."

"I just did what had to be done."

"That's right. You didn't look for the easy way out."

"I did it for our baby."

"I know."

They got out of the car and he walked her to the front door.

"I'll give you a call tomorrow. Let me know what you decide."

"I will."

Mark kissed Jenny good night and saw her safely inside before driving away.

He was smiling.

She had accepted his proposal.

One way or another, they would be married soon.

Darrell was in the warehouse lunchroom when Burke found him.

"What are you reading?"

"I'm thinking about becoming a Catholic. The priest at the church gave me this book."

Burke smiled and sat down across from him. He didn't know if his talking to him about God had been a factor in Darrell's decision, but he was happy for him. "I always knew you were a smart man."

The two laughed easily together.

"I don't know about that."

"I do," Burke said with confidence. "You doing all right?"

Darrell smiled. "I'm fine."

"That's right, and you will be, as long as you've got Jesus." Burke started to get up, ready to go back to work. "No greater love has any man—"

"Than the one who goes back to work on time," Darrell quipped.

"Just make sure it's the Lord's work you're doing," his friend advised as he moved away.

Darrell returned to his reading.

He had to admit he was learning a lot.

"Did you hear the latest?" Officer Anderson was on his way out of headquarters at the end of his shift when he ran into Tom Warren and Bob Phillips.

"No. What happened today?" Phillips asked, expecting bad news.

"They found the car that was used in the drive-by."

"Where?" Warren asked.

"Down by the river."

"Did they learn anything?"

"Not much. It had been torched, and the plates, it turns out, were stolen. We got word to Stan Schmidt, the parole officer, so he could let Darrell Miller know not to let his guard down yet."

"Who's Miller?" Phillips wondered.

"He's the witness from the shooting who gave us the information. It looks like he's going to have to lay low a little while longer."

"I know that name." Phillips frowned. He tried to recall where he'd heard of Darrell Miller before.

"He's an ex-con. He served time for robbery and is back out on the streets."

"Are you sure he didn't do the shooting himself?" Warren asked.

"No, Miller's gone straight. He's staying clean and trying to live the good life."

"Yeah, the good life—just like the rest of us," Phillips said sarcastically, thinking of the ugliness they saw in their jobs day in and day out.

Warren and Phillips headed out on their patrols, and Anderson called it a night.

The first chance Warren got, he stopped at a pay phone to make a call.

"His name's Darrell Miller. Find the bastard and take care of it."

* * *

Margo had deliberately lost herself in work after her confrontation with Mark. She'd stayed late at the office, catching up on everything she'd missed while she'd been away, and hadn't gotten home until after dark.

It was nearly midnight as she sat alone in her living room, lost in thought. She'd managed to avoid dwelling on Mark and Jenny and their baby—until now. Now she had to face the truth.

Mark had made his choice today.

He had chosen Jenny.

He had chosen Jenny over Seton Leasing and over her.

Margo grimaced as she realized how ugly her situation was. She had two choices. She could stand by her original feelings about the situation and not give in, or she could go to Jenny and Mark and try to make amends. If she chose the first way, Margo knew she would lose her son forever. She had seen Grant's strength in him today. Mark was not going to back down or change his mind.

Could she go on living without her son?

Margo didn't know why she even bothered to consider a course that might cause a permanent rift between them. She had devoted her whole life to making Seton Leasing successful just to provide for Mark. She loved him. True, she didn't always agree with him, but she loved him. She could not imagine life without him.

Humbling herself didn't come easy to Margo.

It wasn't often she admitted she'd made a mistake, but this time she'd made a serious one. She'd forgotten how wonderful and how powerful true love was.

Mark loved Jenny.

He was determined to do the right thing by her and their baby.

Their baby—

Facing the fact and accepting it still troubled Margo. She hadn't really thought about the baby before. At the time, all those months ago, she had thought of the pregnancy only as an annoyance, but not anymore. According to Mark, Jenny was due to deliver very soon. Whatever Margo was going to do, she had to do soon.

Margo knew the answer. She had been wrong and she had to admit it—to Jenny and to Mark.

It wouldn't be easy.

But it would be worth it.

Her decision made, Margo went to bed. She wasn't exactly sure how she was going to go about it, but she was certain she would figure something out.

Her last thought as she drifted off to sleep was—*I'm going to be a grandmother.*

CHAPTER TWENTY-THREE
DAY EIGHT

Give Me Peace, O Lord . . .

It was after midnight when the supervisor came to get Darrell where he was working near the docks.

"You got a phone call, Miller."

"Where do you want me to take it?" Darrell was immediately worried. No one had ever called him at work before. Whatever it was about, it had to be important.

"My office is fine."

Darrell hurried to the office in the front of the warehouse to answer the phone.

"Hello?"

"Darrell? This is Stan Schmidt."

For a moment, Darrell felt good about the call. He thought Stan had news for him about the shooter, that there had been an arrest, that the threat was gone.

"I've got some bad news for you."

As fast as the positive thoughts had come, they were gone. "What happened?"

Stan explained how the police had located the car but were unable to get any evidence from it. "Things aren't looking good right now, so be careful."

"I have been," he said in disgust. "Is this ever going to end? Why the hell did I have to be the one who saw them?"

"I'm sorry, Darrell. I wish I could do more. If I hear anything, anything at all, I'll let you know right away."

"Thanks."

Darrell hung up more disgusted and distraught than he'd ever been before.

He'd trusted the cops.

He'd believed they would find the killer.

But no more.

He couldn't live this way, hiding all the time, afraid to leave his house, afraid for Claire. He had to do something, and he had to do it now.

Darrell was determined as he left his boss's office. He did not return to work.

He walked out without telling anyone. He didn't care if they fired him for leaving.

He had to do this.

Darrell headed for his old neighborhood to find Nash and Vince.

The cops had been no help. Maybe his old friends would be.

Two hours later, Darrell was furious and frustrated. He had gone to two all-night bars, but had found no trace of Nash or Vince. He made his way to what he hoped would be his last stop—the strip club where they used to hang out.

Darrell nodded to the guard at the door, who eyed him suspiciously as he walked in. The air reeked with the smell of cigarette smoke and sweaty humanity. He had a pained realization of just how glad he was that Claire had come into his life. Without her loving influence, he would still be living this way, and probably dying this way, too. He went to the bar.

"You look familiar," the bartender said, eyeing him.

"Forgot me already, did you, Rick?" Darrell challenged.

"Miller!" Rick recognized him at last. "When did they let you out?"

"I been back on the streets for some months now, but I'm trying to keep my act clean."

"That ain't no fun. What can I get you?"

"I'll take a beer," Darrell answered.

When he'd been served, Darrell paid the bartender, then took a drink. He looked around as the music began and saw two young women come out on stage and start "dancing" together. He turned away.

"I'm looking for some old friends," he finally told Rick. "You seen anything of Nash and Vince?"

"They're around."

Darrell pulled a ten-dollar bill out of his pocket

and shoved it across the bar. "Where could I find them tonight?"

"Oooh, I like a man who flaunts his money," a honey-toned voice purred.

Darrell tensed as a woman pressed herself fully against him from behind. He turned, trying to shift away from her, but the scantily clad stripper was too quick for him. She linked her arms around his neck and tried to kiss him on the mouth. Determined to be rid of her, Darrell took her by the arms and put her from him.

"You don't like what I'm offering?" the stripper asked, sticking her chest out even farther for him to ogle. She was disappointed when he seemed unaffected by her move.

"I'm not in the mood."

"I could get you in the mood," she promised.

"Get lost."

"What's the matter? Don't you like girls?" the stripper challenged angrily. She was used to men going crazy over her, not turning her down.

"I got a woman at home waiting for me."

"And one woman is enough for you?"

"That's right."

She looked him up and down, then moved away to the next customer—a man who appreciated her beauty and talent.

Darrell looked back at Rick. "You know where they are?"

Rick had already pocketed the money. "Try the pool hall four blocks over."

"Thanks." Darrell took another drink of his

beer and left the club, glad to be outside again. He only hoped Rick was right. He'd wanted to return to work before his shift ended, but at the rate he was going, he wasn't sure he was going to make it.

Darrell saw Nash and Vince the minute he walked into the pool hall.

"Would you look at who just showed up," Nash taunted at his first sight of Darrell. "I wondered how long it would be before you came around to our way of thinking."

Vince looked up at him and smiled. "What are you doing here? I thought you were living the clean life now."

After what he'd already been through trying to find them, Darrell was in no mood for their remarks. "Shut up. I need to talk to you. It's important."

Darrell's tone was so deadly serious, they didn't doubt him for a minute. They both hoped he had changed his mind about working with them again, and had a job planned. They could always use the extra cash.

"Well, come on over to my 'office,'" Vince said, walking to the last booth. He didn't want anyone to overhear them.

Darrell looked at the two men across the table once they were all sitting down. "I need your help."

"What have you got planned?"

"I'm not planning anything." He wanted to convince them of that right away.

"Then what are you doing here?" Nash sneered.

"I need to find whoever shot that store owner last week."

"What's that to you?" Nash wondered.

"Yeah, why are you worrying about him?" Vince asked cautiously. "People get shot here all the time."

"But I'm not a witness all the time," Darrell muttered.

Nash and Vince were both stunned by his revelation.

"Shit, Darrell, you're a dead man!" Nash swore.

"Tell me something I don't know," he snarled.

"What are you going to do?"

"I'm going to get them before they get me, that's what I'm going to do," he said fiercely. "Who is it? Who was the shooter?"

Nash and Vince shared a quick look, and Darrell could tell immediately that they knew something; they were very nervous.

"What do you know? Tell me."

"You want us to end up dead, too?"

"No, man, I want the bastard off the streets. I want him arrested and locked up for the rest of his life."

"How are you going to do that?"

"If the cops arrest him, we'll be safe."

Nash and Vince both laughed harshly.

"The cops? I never thought you were stupid, Darrell," Vince ridiculed.

"What are you talking about?"

"You think the cops are going to help you? You think the cops will find this guy and arrest him?

Hell, man, you're dreaming. The cops are behind it!" Vince revealed the ugly truth.

Darrell froze as he glared at them across the table. "What are you talking about?"

Nash leaned closer and kept his voice low. "There's a cop on the take. He's the one behind all this. He's been putting the squeeze on the store owners to pay up for protection or else. He doesn't do the dirty work himself. He's got his boys running around doing that for him, but he's the one taking the cash and running the show."

Darrell was sickened by the news. No wonder the cops hadn't found the shooter! He had trusted them, but no more.

"Who is he? What's his name?" Darrell demanded. He was ready to immediately contact Stan with what he'd learned.

"We don't know. Everybody's real close-mouthed. Those that ain't end up dead."

Darrell was frustrated that they couldn't tell him more, but at least he was on to something.

"I owe you," Darrell told them both as he got up to leave.

"Damn right, you do," Nash called, watching him as he left the pool hall and disappeared into the dark night. When Darrell had gone, he looked over at Vince. "I just hope the fool stays alive long enough to pay us back."

"So do I."

Darrell was a driven man as he walked away from the pool hall. He needed to contact Stan right away and let him know what he'd found out.

He didn't want to use a pay phone on the street, so he went back to work. He knew his supervisor wouldn't be happy with him for walking out, but that didn't matter right now. What mattered was getting the news to Stan as fast as he could.

"Where the hell have you been, Miller?" the supervisor demanded after cussing him out when he returned to the warehouse.

"I had some personal business I had to take care of."

"You don't just walk off the job here without checking with me! Get your ass back to your pay point, now!"

"I have to make a call first," Darrell said.

"Like hell you do."

"No, I need to call my parole officer."

"If you don't get your ass back to your pay point and stay there, I'll be the one calling your parole officer to get your parole revoked! You've been gone for hours without a word! Who the hell do you think you are? You're damned lucky I'm not firing you right now!"

Darrell realized there was nothing he could do but go back to work. As desperate as he was to talk to Schmidt, he knew it wasn't going to happen until he got off. Resigned to waiting a little longer, he returned to work.

The hours passed slowly. Darrell thought his shift would never end, but finally it did.

"You make sure you show up on time tomorrow night, Miller, and don't even think about walking out of here ever again," his boss ordered.

Darrell only nodded as he left. He was cautious on the streets on his way to Our Lady. He didn't even consider using a pay phone. It was almost daylight, and he didn't want to be on the streets. He hoped Father Walters would be the priest saying Mass this morning. If he was, Darrell was certain he would allow him to use the phone in the church office. He had to get in touch with Schmidt now.

Darrell entered Our Lady through the front door. He could see lights on in the small room off the welcoming area and went to see if the priest was there. To his relief, Father Walters was there, getting ready for Mass.

"Father—"

The priest looked up, surprised by the interruption.

"Good morning, Darrell."

"Is there a phone around I could use? It's important or I wouldn't bother you."

"It's not a problem. Go through that door into the back office," he directed. "There's a phone on the desk there."

"Thanks."

"Is there anything I can help you with?"

"You already have."

Darrell went in the room and closed the door. He quickly dialed Schmidt's home phone number and waited tensely for him to answer.

"Yeah, this is Schmidt," Stan said in a sleep-groggy voice.

"This is Miller."

Stan was instantly alert. "What's wrong?"

269

"Nothing's wrong. I think something's right for a change."

"What are you talking about?"

"I did some checking around on my own tonight and found out that there's a cop on the take. Word on the street says he's the one behind the shootings."

"What?" Stan sat up in bed.

"You heard me."

"Who is it?" Stan asked, bracing himself for the bad news.

"No one's talking, but it's a fact."

"You trust the person who told you this?"

"Yes." There was no doubt in his mind the information was accurate. Nash and Vince had no reason to lie.

"I'll take care of it. You watch out for yourself."

"Don't worry. I will."

"I'll be in touch."

Darrell came out of the back room to find that Mass had already started. He entered the church and took a seat near the back. He prayed fervently for an end to his troubles. The killer was still on the loose, but would the cops bring him in if the man behind the murder was one of their own?

Darrell did not leave during Communion this morning. He stayed in his pew until Father Walters proclaimed Mass ended and left the church. Then Darrell followed him out.

"Is everything all right, Darrell?" Father Walters asked, seeing how serious he looked as he walked by.

"Not really."

"Do you need to talk?" he offered.

"No, no. Just keep praying for me," he answered. "I did want to let you know that the cops found the shooter's car, but they couldn't get any evidence off of it."

Darrell wanted to tell him about the bad cop, too, but there were other parishioners standing around nearby, waiting for the chance to talk to the priest, too. Darrell didn't want to be overheard, so he decided to wait until a more private time to tell him that news.

"That's too bad. I wish they'd get a break in this case."

"So do I."

"Well, I will keep you in my prayers."

"Thanks, Father.

"You might want to have a talk with Saint Michael. He's the patron saint of policemen. Maybe he can inspire them to solve this case."

"They need help, that's for sure," he remarked, wondering what Saint Michael would do to a corrupt killer cop. Judging from the pictures he'd seen of the powerful archangel, sword in hand, Darrell knew it wouldn't be pretty.

"Be careful out there," the priest urged.

"I will."

"You'll be stopping by the rectory one afternoon so we can discuss the chapters you've read, won't you?"

"How's Friday?"

"I'll be looking forward to it."

Darrell left Our Lady, taking care to check the street in both directions. All seemed calm, so he started for the safety of his home—and Claire.

CHAPTER TWENTY-FOUR

Mark was surprised his mother's parking space was empty when he arrived at work the next day, but he didn't worry about it. He knew she would show up eventually, and if she wanted to see him, she would know where to find him.

"Good morning, Joanne," Mark greeted her, his good mood evident.

"Is it?" she asked cautiously, wondering what had happened since he'd walked out the day before.

"It most definitely is." He stopped before her desk. "Jenny accepted my proposal."

"Congratulations!" she said delightedly.

"I am a lucky man."

"I think she's a lucky girl."

"That's why I pay you the big bucks," Mark laughed.

"Why? Because I always tell the truth?"

He was still laughing as he went into his office

to get to work. He needed to be caught up in case Jenny decided they should go for their marriage license that afternoon.

It was several hours later when the door to his office opened and his mother strode in.

"I see you're back," Margo said in her most managerial tone.

"And hard at work." He leaned back and looked up at her as she stood before his desk.

There was tension between them as they faced each other.

"We need to talk," she told him.

"I think you said it all yesterday," he said tersely, remembering their conversation far too clearly.

"No, I didn't. There are a few more things we need to discuss."

"I told you—"

"I'm very aware of what you told me, Mark. I listened to you yesterday, and now it's your turn to listen to me." She stepped forward and held out an envelope to him. "Here."

Mark thought she'd handed him his walking papers.

His expression turned grim.

He could start a new career somewhere else, but his main concern was providing for Jenny and their child.

He opened the envelope.

Instead of a pink slip, Mark pulled out a gift certificate from the most expensive, exclusive baby store in town. He stared down at the amount written there in disbelief. "What's this?"

"It's a present for my grandchild. I didn't know what Jenny needed, so I thought a gift certificate was best."

Mark slowly stood up, his gaze meeting and holding his mother's. "You're not firing me?"

"Did you honestly think I'd let you off that easily? There's too much work to do around here. You can't leave Seton Leasing. You *are* Seton Leasing."

"What about Jenny—and our baby?" He had to ask. He had to know how she felt.

"Oh, sweetheart—" Margo's business manner vanished completely, and she turned into a mother who loved her son. She went to him and took him in her arms.

Mark stood for a moment, uncertain as she embraced him.

"I'm sorry, Mark. More than you'll ever know—I'm sorry." Her words were heartfelt.

He put his arms around her in return, relieved.

"I love you, Mark. Can you forgive me? Yesterday I told you you were a fool, but now I realize I was the fool."

Mark knew what a proud woman his mother was. For her to apologize and ask his forgiveness was truly amazing. "Of course I forgive you, Mom. I love you, too."

They moved apart.

Margo looked up at him, tears burning in her

eyes. She'd been afraid that too much damage had been done to their relationship to save it, and now relief flooded through her. "I need to apologize to Jenny, too. Is there a time when we could meet and I could make amends?"

"I'll call and ask."

"Good. The sooner we straighten things out between us, the better."

"I know. She's going to be your daughter-in-law soon."

"What?"

"Yes. She accepted my proposal last night. We're going to be married as soon as we can arrange it."

"That's wonderful." Margo was honestly happy for him.

"I think so, too."

"What are you planning to do for the wedding?"

"We're going to work that out today." He related what they'd learned from Father Walters at church.

"It's good that her church is so serious about marriage, but you don't want your baby born out of wedlock, do you?"

"No, we don't."

"I guess it will have to be a civil ceremony, then, if you're to get married before the baby is born," Margo said thoughtfully, wondering what she could do to help.

"Yes."

"Would you like to come to the house for dinner tonight? Or could we go out to eat somewhere nice and talk about it?"

"I'll ask Jenny when I speak with her."

"Good, and let me know." Margo reached up and pressed an adoring kiss to her son's cheek.

Mark watched her as she started to leave.

"Mom?"

Margo looked back questioningly.

"Thank you."

They shared a smile.

Then they both went back to work.

They had a successful company to run.

"A toast to us," Paige said, lifting her coffee cup to Dorothy in salute.

"Yes, to Total Elegance," Dorothy agreed.

They touched their coffee cups and then each took a sip to make it official.

"I wish I had some champagne, but if I start drinking this early, I won't get a lot done today." Paige was smiling. "The fashion show really worked for us."

"Yes, it did."

"It was our best weekend ever! Our business is only going to get better from here on out. You are my good luck charm, Dorothy."

"I don't know about that, but thank you for the compliment."

"How's your grandson?"

"Much better."

"Thank heaven." Paige looked at her sympathetically. "For all that we had a great week-end here at the store, you had a tough one at home."

"Yes, I did." Dorothy grimaced. "It was difficult enough with Nick being sick, but having Alan there at the hospital with me was really hard, especially after running into Tina the other day."

"How did you handle it?"

Her grimace changed to an almost confident half-smile. "Actually, I surprised myself. I think I did rather well. He tried to question me about money, and I told him to talk to my attorney."

"That's the best way to handle it."

"I know. The less time I spend with him, the better. My daughter called and told me he stopped by her place for a while. I guess Tina must have been busy if he had time to go see Carol."

"You are so bad," Paige teased.

Dorothy's expression turned thoughtful. "The one good thing that has come out of this situation is that it's helped me to figure out who I am. All my life I've been either somebody's daughter or somebody's wife or somebody's mom. Now, finally, I'm me. And I like it. I like it a lot. I didn't know I could be this brave or this daring. I'm proud of myself."

"You should be. You're a smart woman."

"Thanks."

"What will you do if your husband realizes he was wrong to leave you?"

Dorothy frowned. "I don't even want to think about that. Right now, I don't know that I'd take him back—not that he'll be coming back. We've both seen Tina. I don't think he'll give her up."

"She was one hot twenty-something, that's for sure."

"You know, now that I think about it, today is Alan's birthday. I wonder if Tina is going to throw him a big birthday party."

"Nobody would come," Paige quipped.

"You're right, and besides, what is Tina going to think about his being another year older? I should forward his mail to him more often, so Tina could see all the letters he gets from AARP!"

Paige laughed out loud. "You go, girl!"

The UPS guy came into the shop with a delivery, and Dorothy was glad for the distraction. Putting out exciting new outfits was much more fun than thinking about "old" Alan.

Alan sat at his desk, staring at his calendar, wondering how things had ended up this way.

It was his birthday.

There had always been a party. Every year, Dorothy arranged for the whole family to gather around. There would be cake and ice cream, and presents and laughter.

And there would be love.

Love—

Memories assailed him—memories of times now bittersweet to him.

Alan forced them away.

That was the past.

His secretary had already brought him today's mail, and he hadn't gotten one card—not one.

No one had remembered.

No one had cared.

He smiled grimly.

There was no one else to look to or blame. It was his own fault.

Finally and regretfully, Alan accepted that he had made a grievous mistake in giving in to his desire for Tina. He had forsaken his entire life for her. He had betrayed Dorothy and Carol and David. He had thrown away everything—and for what?

Misery pounded at him—misery and disgust with his own weakness.

Alan wondered if Adam had felt this way after eating the apple. He'd blown it big time, and he had no one else to blame.

Had it been worth it? Had that time with Tina been worth destroying his very existence?

He knew the answer. He had been self-centered and selfish. He'd never given a thought to the pain his actions would cause others. He'd been arrogant, never considering the repercussions of giving in to his lust for Tina.

Lust—

Alan smiled wryly as he remembered the religion teacher he'd had in grade school, who'd taught him about the seven deadly sins. Good old lust was one of them. She'd been right. They were deadly.

Alan tried to recall the other six, and finally the lesson learned so long ago came back to him— lust, greed, pride, sloth, envy, gluttony and anger. Thinking of them, he realized he'd fallen for more than just one of them. He'd been proud, too, believing that what he wanted was the most important thing in the world.

Humility swept over him, and, feeling very much like a twelve-year-old again, Alan realized, painfully, what he had to do.

He got out the phone book and looked up the number for Our Lady.

Alan hoped one of the priests would have time for him today. He needed to talk to someone. He needed help. It took all the courage he could muster just to dial the number.

As he realized his cowardice, he gave a short, derisive laugh. He'd never hesitated when calling Tina.

It had been easy to sin.

Sin had been exciting—at the time.

Atoning for it was going to be something else.

Alan's grip on the receiver tightened as the call went through.

Mark and Jenny walked out of the courthouse smiling. They had just gotten their marriage license and had arranged to be married in a civil ceremony by a justice of the peace on Saturday.

"I'm glad we're doing this," Mark told her.

They climbed in his car, and he started to drive them back toward work.

"So am I, but I still want to go through the marriage prep program at church."

"Don't worry. We will," he assured her.

"You don't mind marrying me twice?" she teased.

Mark looked over at her. "Jenny, I'll marry you every week, if that's what you want."

Her heartbeat quickened at the look in his eyes. "I love you."

"I love you, too, and after this Saturday, we'll never be apart again."

Jenny sighed and smiled.

"Are you all right about having dinner with my mother tonight?"

"Yes. It's not going to be easy, but I know we have to do it." The meeting with her future mother-in-law couldn't be avoided forever. The sooner she got it over with, the better things would be for everyone involved.

"Thank you. What time do you want me to pick you up?"

"I should be ready by six."

"I'll be there," he promised as he pulled up to the curb at Jenny's office to drop her off.

"I'll be waiting," she told him as she got out of the car.

Jenny stood on the sidewalk, watching Mark drive away, then went back to work. She had a feeling the rest of the afternoon was going to pass a lot more quickly than she wanted it to. As much as she wanted to spend every waking, breathing moment with Mark, the last thing she wanted to do was be with his mother. The evening to come was going to be horribly awkward at best.

CHAPTER TWENTY-FIVE

Sergeant Williams stood with Officer Anderson in his office, the door closed to ensure the privacy of their conversation. He had just revealed to Anderson what he'd learned earlier that day from Stan Schmidt about the bad cop.

"But who could it be?" Anderson was clearly shocked by the news.

"If I knew that, he'd already be locked up."

Anderson frowned. "I haven't heard or seen anything unusual around headquarters."

"Neither have I. So whoever it is, he's good—real good. I've initiated an internal investigation, but until we catch him, I want you to help me stay on Miller 24/7."

"Done."

"We have to keep a low profile. We don't want anyone to know we're around."

"What's Miller's schedule?"

Sergeant Williams handed him his file on the ex-con. "He works the late-night shift at the warehouse, so it should be simple to keep an eye on him while he's coming and going."

"Good." Anderson checked over the information. "We could use some breaks on this case."

"Keep your ears open. If you hear anything—anything at all that sounds suspicious—let me know immediately, and don't tell anyone else what we're doing."

"Right. I'll head out now and keep an eye on Miller's home."

"I'll relieve you. Don't trust anybody, unless you hear from me first."

"Got it."

"And take an unmarked car. This is serious."

Audrey, the secretary at Our Lady's rectory, looked up from her desk as the door opened.

"Why, Alan, it's good to see you. What can I do for you today?"

"Hello, Audrey. I have an appointment with Father Walters."

"All right, let me give him a call and see if he's ready for you."

She went to her desk and dialed the priest's extension. She spoke quickly with him, then hung up.

"You can go on back. His office is the third door on the left."

"Thanks, Audrey."

Alan couldn't believe he was nervous as he walked down the narrow hallway toward Father

Walters's private office. He hadn't felt this way about going to confession since grade school, but at least then, his sins hadn't been so horrendous. He wondered miserably, even if God did forgive him, would he be able to forgive himself?

The office door was closed when he reached it. He knocked once and waited.

"Come in," Father Walters called out.

Alan opened the door and let himself in.

"Please, sit down." The priest indicated the chair opposite his desk. "What can I do for you today?"

Alan slid into the chair and glanced around, feeling decidedly uneasy. Finally he looked up, faced Father Walters and admitted, "I need to go to confession."

"All right," the priest said quietly.

"Father, forgive me for I have sinned," Alan said awkwardly, not recalling the full Act of Contrition he'd learned as a child.

"How long has it been since your last confession?"

"At least ten years."

"Go on," Father Walters encouraged, wanting to help him in any way he could. He realized it had taken a lot of courage on Alan's part to come to him this way.

Alan drew a deep breath.

"I committed adultery," he confessed.

There, Alan thought, *I've said it*.

"I was selfish and stupid," he went on. "I even went so far as to tell Dorothy I wanted a divorce—"

Father remained silent, but he was surprised by this news. He often saw Dorothy at church, and she hadn't spoken to him about the situation.

"I've destroyed my life and everything I've ever worked for."

"Are you truly sorry for what you've done?"

"Oh, yes." His remorse was real, all right. "If I could turn back the clock, I would—in an instant."

"You can't change what's already happened," the priest advised, "but you can make the decision to change your future for the better. Are you willing to do that?"

Alan nodded, looking suitably chastened. "Yes, Father. I realize what a fool I've been."

"Then start now to atone for your sins. For your penance, try to help those you've hurt. Show them you've changed. Ask them for their forgiveness."

"I don't know if I can forgive myself. How can I expect my wife and kids to forgive me?"

"God forgives you," Father Walters said solemnly.

Alan drew a ragged breath. "I'll do my best."

Father Walters began solemnly, "God, the Father of mercies, through the death and resurrection of His Son has reconciled the world to Himself and sent the Holy Spirit upon us for forgiveness of sins; through the ministry of the Church may God give you pardon and peace. I forgive and absolve you in the name of the Father, and of the Son and of the Holy Spirit. Amen."

"Amen," Alan repeated with meaning. "Thank you, Father."

He nodded. "Is there anything else I can help you with?"

"Just pray for me. I'm going to need all the prayers I can get with what I have to face now."

"I will," Father Walters promised.

Alan stood and shook his hand. He started to leave the office.

"Alan—" Father Walters called out to him.

Alan looked back.

"Good luck."

"What do you mean, you haven't found Miller yet?" Warren exploded to Eddie, his gunman. "Find the son of a bitch! That's what I pay you for!"

"I've been asking around and checking places," Eddie responded hotly. "Rick, the bartender at the strip club, says Miller was in the other night. It was the first time he'd seen him in a long time. Rick said Miller was looking for some old friends—two men named Vince and Nash. I've got the word out on the street to find them, too."

"Stay on it."

Before Eddie could say more, the phone went dead in his hand.

"I should have given this to you earlier, but I forgot," Mark said. He handed Jenny the envelope from his mother as he drove them to her house that evening.

"What is it?"

"Open it and see."

"Who gave you this?" Her eyes widened as she saw the size of the gift certificate.

"It's from my mother."

"But it's so much—"

"My mother never does anything halfway. She's sorry for all that's happened, and she wants to make things right."

Jenny looked at Mark. "You've already done that."

He slanted her a quick smile. "Good, then things won't be too rough for you tonight."

"I hope not."

"Are you ready?" he asked as he pulled into the driveway and parked.

"As I'll ever be," Jenny said, girding herself.

Mark helped her out of the car. Together, they started up the walk. As they neared the front door, it opened and Margo came out.

"Hello, Jenny." Margo watched Jenny coming toward her, heavy with child.

"Mrs. Seton."

"Come on in." She stood back to let them go inside.

"Is dinner ready?" Mark asked, deliberately wanting to distract the two women in his life.

"Ready and waiting. I knew you two would be hungry."

"What are we having?" Mark asked. It smelled like an Italian restaurant in the house.

"I heard talk that someone thinks pizza is the world's best food, so I tried my hand at pizza."

"We're having pizza?" Jenny knew Mrs. Seton was a gourmet cook, and she was surprised that she would even consider making pizza.

"Just for you," Margo said with a gentle smile. "Let's eat."

She put an arm around Jenny and closed the door behind them.

Claire cuddled next to Darrell on their sofa. Ever since he'd told her what had happened the night before, she'd been worrying about him. A terrible sense of foreboding gripped her.

"I don't want you to go to work tonight. Stay here with me."

"Baby, there is nothing I'd like better than to stay right here." Darrell emphasized his words with a passionate kiss. "But after last night, I'm lucky to still have a job. I gotta go in. If I don't—"

"I know," she conceded reluctantly. "We don't want to do anything to mess up your parole."

"That's right." He kissed her again. "I've been thinking—"

"That's dangerous," she murmured against his lips.

"Yes, it is, because I've been thinking it's time we got married."

Claire drew back to stare up at him in complete surprise. "What?"

"It's time, love," he went on. "Plan it any way you want, but let's do it."

"Oh, Darrell!" Her dream had come true. She'd been hoping and praying they'd spend the rest of their lives together. "I love you!"

He kissed her passionately one last time, then reluctantly pulled away and got up.

"Any more kissing like that, and I will be out of a job. I gotta go. I'll see you in the morning."

"I'll be waiting for you."

"That's what I'm counting on."

He left the apartment building and started off for work.

Tom Warren waited around at headquarters after his shift ended. He acted like he was taking care of business, but in reality he was just biding his time until things got quiet there and traffic thinned out. Once he was reasonably sure no one would question him, he made his way to Sergeant Williams's office.

Warren knew his sergeant was gone for the night, so Warren figured it was as safe as it would ever be to try to find information about Miller. He started on the desk top and went through all the file folders stacked there, but to no avail. He grew more tense as he searched through the desk drawers. Finally he found what he was looking for—a folder secreted away in the bottom drawer. Warren scanned the contents quickly. There wasn't a lot there, but it did contain Miller's home address and place of work.

Warren put everything back where it belonged. He left the office unobserved. No one ever knew he was there.

CHAPTER TWENTY-SIX
DAY NINE

No Greater Gift. . .

Alan passed a restless night. No matter what he tried, he couldn't sleep. Thoughts of Dorothy and his family played in his mind, rendering any chance of rest impossible. Finally, as 5:30 A.M. came and went, he knew what he had to do. He turned off his alarm, set to go off at six, and got up.

Dorothy generally attended 6:30 Mass. He would seek her out there and see if she would talk with him for a few minutes.

It was worth a try.

He certainly had nothing to lose, and everything to gain.

"You want a ride?" Burke offered as he and Darrell got ready to leave work.

"Sure. Thanks." He was beginning to believe Burke was his guardian angel in disguise. He'd been feeling uneasy all night long, and this offer of a ride was really welcome.

They climbed into his car and drove off the lot.

"Where you headed? Church?"

"Yeah."

"How's the studying going?"

"It's interesting, but I didn't get a lot read today. I'm meeting with the priest on Friday to go over whatever I do get finished."

"It takes strength to realize you need the Lord."

"There's no doubt about that. I've tried going it alone, and it ain't pretty."

"I'm with you on that. I'd have been dead by now if I hadn't cleaned up my act."

"Well, I'm glad you did, 'cause I appreciate these rides."

They both managed a laugh, tired as they were.

Burke stopped the car by the side entrance of the church to let Darrell out.

"Thanks for the lift."

"No problem. See you tonight."

Darrell glanced quickly around. Nothing seemed out of the ordinary. All was quiet, and that was good. He went inside.

Sergeant Williams was tired. He'd kept watch all night outside the warehouse. Finally Miller had walked out and gotten into a car with another worker.

Williams followed the car, but stayed back far enough not to arouse suspicion. He was surprised when the car pulled to a stop by the Catholic church and Miller got out. Williams watched him go in, presumably to attend the 6:30 Mass that was about to start.

A fallen-away Catholic himself, Williams knew he had half an hour before Mass was over. He parked down the street, where he had a good view of the front and side entrances.

For a moment, Williams thought about attending Mass, too, but he decided to stay in the car. He didn't want to risk the church ceiling falling in on him.

Williams smiled at his own humor, then got serious again.

He settled in to wait and watch.

Dorothy was in a good mood this morning. She entered Our Lady and started down the main aisle to her regular pew. She smiled at the young man whose name she didn't know, but whom she'd seen there regularly at Mass the past week or so. Jenny Emerson was there, too, and Dorothy gave her a big smile as she passed her. She nodded to Joe Myers, then genuflected and entered her pew.

Kneeling down to pray, Dorothy concentrated on giving thanks for all the good things in her life—for Nick's health, for Total Elegance, for her children's love and support. Out of the corner of her eye, she noticed someone enter the pew across the aisle from her. When she'd finished offering her prayers, she sat back and glanced over to see who had come in. She froze.

It was Alan!

What was he doing there?

Anger filled her instantly.

Can't I even go to Mass in peace?

Dorothy was tempted to choke him, but controlled the urge. Violence in church was frowned upon.

Forcing herself to calm down, she focused on the altar.

She offered up a desperate prayer for strength.

It looked like she was going to need it today.

"I saw Miller! I was ready! I coulda had him!" Eddie snarled in frustration to Wayne, his partner driving the car. Warren had called earlier to tell him where Miller worked, and he had been there, ready and waiting, at shift change. "If the son of a bitch hadn't gotten in that car, I could have shot him down in the parking lot!"

"What do you want to do now? We can't just keep driving around in circles waiting for him to come out of church," Wayne said.

They'd followed the car and had seen Miller get out and go in the church. It had happened so fast, Eddie had had no opportunity to get off a shot at him then.

"Church—" Eddie sneered. "What the hell is he doing in church?"

Wayne laughed coldly. "Don't you know? He's getting ready to die."

They shared a look.

"You're right, my man. He is." Eddie studied

the neighborhood. It was just getting light. "Go ahead and pull into the church parking lot."

Wayne did as he was told. He found a quiet place to park where they could wait for the service to end.

"When he comes out, be ready. You drive fast. I want to be long gone before anybody realizes what happened."

Jenny found herself smiling all through Mass. She was still having a hard time believing that last night had really happened. Mrs. Seton—Margo, as she'd asked Jenny to call her—had been truly nice. She had even apologized for what had happened before and asked for her forgiveness. Jenny understood how difficult it must have been for her, for Margo was a proud woman. When she'd been leaving, Margo had come up to her and given her a hug. Instinctively, Jenny had hugged her back. It wouldn't be easy for Jenny to completely forget what had transpired between them earlier, but Margo seemed honest in her apology and in her interest in the baby.

The baby—

God certainly worked miracles.

Jenny would never have believed a few weeks ago that her life could have changed so dramatically.

But it had.

Mark loved her.

They were going to be married in just a few short days.

Life was good.

* * *

Eddie and Wayne sat in the car, waiting.

"Why do these people want to go to church on a weekday? It's bad enough you're supposed to go on Sunday," Wayne mocked the faithful.

"They must be real bored," Eddie derided.

"They won't be for long," Wayne chuckled evilly.

"Things are going to get exciting here very shortly."

"You ready?"

"Oh, yeah."

Eddie checked his gun again just to make sure, and he smiled with confidence. He was going to enjoy calling Warren and giving him the news that the job was done.

"Mass is ended. Let us go in peace to love and serve the Lord," Father Walters said.

"Thanks be to God," the parishioners responded.

Once the priest had left the church, everyone else started to file out.

Dorothy did not want to talk to Alan, so she tried to make a quick escape down the side aisle.

Alan understood what she was doing, but he desperately wanted to speak with her. Talking to Father Walters yesterday had convinced him it was important he let Dorothy know he was sorry for what he'd done. He hurried•after her and managed to catch up as she went out the front door.

"Dorothy, wait a minute!"

She stopped on the top step and turned to face him. "What do you want?"

"I want to talk to you for a few minutes."

"Why?"

"Because it's important."

"I really don't think we have much to say to one another."

Joe stopped to talk with Father, and Jenny waved to them both as she headed outside, ready to go to work. She was a bit surprised when the man she knew as Darrell was suddenly there, holding the door for her.

"Thanks." Jenny smiled at him.

"No problem," Darrell told her.

"Your name's Darrell, right?"

He nodded, impressed that she'd remembered his name. "And you're Jenny."

"Yes."

"You take care of yourself and your baby."

"I'm trying," she laughed and started down the front church steps just ahead of him.

Eddie caught sight of Miller the minute he stepped out of the church.

"Go! That's him!" Eddie ordered, rolling down his window.

Wayne pulled out of the parking lot. He drove the speed limit, not wanting to draw undue attention to themselves. There would be time enough to floor the pedal, once Eddie had gotten his job done.

Eddie was smiling grimly. Everything was going to work out just fine. He lifted his gun and got ready to aim out the car window.

Sergeant Williams was keeping careful watch, and he saw Darrell Miller leave the church with a pregnant woman. He didn't know who the woman was, and he didn't care. He turned on the ignition and got ready to follow him at a distance.

Anderson was due to relieve him in another hour, so he just had to make sure Miller got safely home and then he could call it a night—or a day, he thought wryly. He was exhausted, but nothing mattered but keeping Miller alive, and identifying the bad cop.

Darrell paused on the steps to look up and down the street. He saw nothing unusual. The only traffic was the few cars pulling out of the church parking lot.

He started to follow Jenny down the steps as a dark sedan pulled out and drove past the church.

He thought nothing of it at first.

He figured it was a parishioner leaving after Mass.

Until he saw that the passenger side window was rolled down—in spite of the cold weather.

Darrell stood unmoving for an instant.

As he watched, the car picked up speed. The man in the passenger's seat stuck his arm out the window. He had a gun in his hand, and it was aimed at Darrell.

Darrell wanted to run, to try to get back inside the church, but the very pregnant Jenny was almost right in front of him.

His only thought was that Jenny would be shot—

"Get down!" he shouted.

Jenny was shocked by Darrell's ferocious yell. She turned toward him in confusion, just as he launched himself at her. She cried out in terror as he pushed her down on the stone steps.

Darrell threw himself upon Jenny, covering her body with his own, wanting to shield her and her baby from harm.

Shots rang out, shattering the quiet of the neighborhood.

And shattering Darrell's life as well.

The well-aimed bullets pierced his body.

Darrell collapsed and rolled limply off Jenny, to lie sprawled on the steps.

CHAPTER TWENTY-SEVEN

Eddie saw the impact of his shots and smiled thinly to himself. He pulled his arm back in the car and rolled up the window.

"Get out of here!" he ordered.

Wayne floored it.

"Shit!" Eddie suddenly swore, looking back over his shoulder to see what was happening.

"What? Did you miss him?"

"Hell, no, I didn't miss him! It's a damned cop! I don't know where in the hell he was, but he's after us!"

"A cop?"

Wayne glanced in his rearview mirror. He swore aloud at the sight of the unmarked cop car speeding up behind them. Its one light was flashing and its siren was roaring.

Wayne ran a red light at a busy intersection, hoping the cross-traffic would block the policeman from following. The oncoming cars swerved wildly to avoid hitting Eddie and Wayne and, in doing so, cleared the way for the cop car in pursuit.

"Move it! He's still on us!" Eddie yelled, panicked now that the cop car was closing on them.

Behind them, Sergeant Williams was grim in his determination. He wasn't about to let them escape He'd already called in the shooting at the church and the need for an ambulance. He'd called for a backup in his chase, too. These two could try to run, but they were going to find out they had nowhere to go and nowhere to hide.

They weren't going to lose him.

He was bringing them in.

Father Walters and Joe had heard what sounded like a car backfiring, but had thought nothing of it. Neither man had realized there was trouble until Dorothy came running back inside screaming.

"Father! Help! A man's been shot!" She was nearly hysterical.

A terrible sense of dread filled Father Walters.
Darrell—

"Joe! Call 911!" he ordered.

Father ran to the door and opened it to find a scene of utter chaos on the steps and street below. People were running and crying out in terror. Halfway down the steps lay Darrell, unconscious and bleeding from his wounds. Jenny was kneeling beside him, trying to help. Alan and several other parishioners were there, too.

"What happened?" Father Walters asked as he rushed to join them.

"I don't know—" Jenny was trembling as she hovered over Darrell. She had taken off her woolen neck scarf and was pressing it against his wounds, trying to stop the bleeding. "We had just started down the steps when all of a sudden Darrell yelled 'Get down!' and then he knocked me down on the steps."

"It was a drive-by, Father!" Alan exclaimed as Dorothy came to stand at his side. "Dorothy and I saw the whole thing."

Father Walters knelt down beside Darrell and quickly checked his pulse. It was weak and unsteady. "He's still alive."

Jenny looked at the priest, her relief obvious. "Thank God! He can't die! He can't!"

"This man saved her life," Alan added.

"Yes, he did," she said, starting to cry.

"There's already a police car in pursuit of the shooter," Alan told Father Walters.

"Good. Joe's calling 911 now. The ambulance should be here any minute."

Even as he spoke, they could hear a siren in the distance.

"Is there anything we can do to help?" Alan and the others offered.

"Alan, go inside and bring me some holy water," Father Walters directed. He remembered Darrell's desire to be baptized.

Alan rushed off to do his bidding.

Jenny was glad when Father Walters took over holding the compress on Darrell's wounds. She sat back weakly on the steps, shaken and almost on the verge of collapse.

Dorothy sat down beside her and put a comforting arm around her. "Are you all right?"

Jenny sagged against her as she fought for control over her emotions. She stared down at the sight of Darrell's blood on her hands and coat. "I don't know."

Joe came running out of the church, passing Alan on his way in. "The ambulance is on its way. How is he?"

"He's alive," Father Walters answered.

Joe went to Jenny. He could see her distress. "Were you hurt?"

"I don't think so—" she answered in a weak voice, feeling only numb.

"Let's move away from here," Joe encouraged. He helped her to her feet and drew her away from the bloody scene. "Do you want to go inside?"

"No—I have to make sure Darrell is going to be all right."

Joe helped her sit down on a step and stayed with her to await the ambulance's arrival.

"I think the EMTs should take a look at you, too. From what I heard, you had quite a fall," he said.

Alan came back out of Our Lady, carrying one of the small bowls of holy water from the vestibule. "Here, Father."

Father Walters took the holy water from him and quickly baptized Darrell. Just as he finished, the ambulance arrived and, with it, a police car.

The EMTs took over.

Everyone backed away to give them the room they needed to work on Darrell. The small group looked on as the men feverishly tried to save him.

"Get the stretcher," one EMT ordered his partner.

As the other man ran to get it from the ambulance, Jenny stood up.

"Will he be all right? Is he going to make it?" she asked.

"We'll do our best." The EMT looked up at her. "Are you all right, ma'am? Do you need to go to the hospital?"

"No, no. Just take care of Darrell. Save him, please—" she begged.

"Are you family?" the man asked.

"No."

"Does anyone know his name or address?"

"Darrell Miller," Father Walters answered, and he told them the rest of what he knew about him.

"Thanks. We'll take it from here."

As they lifted Darrell onto the stretcher, he groaned and opened his eyes. "What—?"

Father Walters was there immediately. "You've been shot, Darrell. They're taking you to the hospital."

"Jenny—how's Jenny?" he whispered.

"You saved her. She's safe."

He gave a weak nod.

"You're going to make it," Father Walters asserted firmly.

Darrell gazed up at the priest, his expression tortured. "Tell Claire"—drawing on the last of his strength, he whispered hoarsely—"tell her I love her."

His eyes closed and he went limp.

The EMTs rushed to get him into the ambulance, and then the parishioners watched as the ambulance sped away toward the hospital.

The police officer who'd responded to Joe's call joined Father Walters on the steps. He began to interview the witnesses, wanting to get information about the crime.

"That bastard is never going to give up!" Wayne snarled. He was driving like a madman through the city streets, desperately trying to lose the cop on their tail. No matter how hard he tried, he could not shake him.

"Shut up and drive!" Eddie ordered. He didn't know how everything had gotten so screwed up, but it had. He still had his gun, but at the speed they were traveling, there was no way he could get off any accurate shots at the cop.

Behind them, Williams concentrated on staying on their tail. These two lowlifes were good, real good, at trying to get away, but it wasn't going to happen. He would not give up until he had them in custody.

Wayne raced on at eighty miles an hour, ignoring all stop signs and cross traffic.

The impact, when it came, was devastating.

A large delivery truck with the right of way broadsided Wayne and Eddie's car on the driver's side. Their vehicle careened across the street and crashed into a lamppost.

Sergeant Williams was on the scene immediately. He quickly parked his car and got out, drawing his gun. He cautiously approached the wrecked car.

"Stay back!" he ordered as a crowd started to gather.

Williams could tell that the driver would be offering him no resistance. The man had gone through the windshield and was hanging there, unconscious, half in the car and half on the hood. As Williams closed on the passenger's side, though, he saw some movement.

"Hold your hands up where I can see them!" he directed.

Eddie was battered and bleeding. He was stunned by what had happened. He heard the cop's order, but wasn't about to give up without a fight. He had just started to turn and lift his gun out the window when he found himself staring down the barrel of the officer's weapon.

"Don't even think about it," Williams ordered in his most deadly voice.

It was over.

Eddie knew it.

He let his gun drop from his hand.

The patrol car Sergeant Williams had called for as backup arrived, and he was grateful to see it was manned by Recca and Hall. He knew them and trusted them. Recca went to check on the truck-driver, while Hall came to assist Williams in making the arrest. Together, they got the shooter out of the car and down on the ground, and Williams handcuffed him. He took his gun as evidence.

"We called for an ambulance," Hall told him.

"How's the truckdriver?" Williams asked Recca when he joined them.

"He's shaken up, but he'll be fine."

"Good." Williams nodded. He quickly explained what had happened. "Take this one in and book him. I have to get back to the scene of the shooting."

"We'll see you down at headquarters."

Williams hurried back to his car. He had to find out how Miller was.

The drive back to the church seemed to take forever as the tension within him grew and grew.

He had been trying to keep Miller safe from harm, and now he feared the worst.

He feared Miller was dead.

Alan was shaken. The violence he'd witnessed had affected him deeply, and the fact that he and Dorothy had almost been caught up in it had completely unnerved him. It made him realize what could have happened. It made him realize, too, how quickly things could change.

Dorothy might have been killed in the shooting. The thought was devastating to him, and he finally understood how much she really meant to him.

Wanting to be near her, Alan made his way over to stand with her and Jenny and Joe.

"We need to talk," Alan told Dorothy in a quiet voice.

"I know." Their gazes met. She turned to Jenny to ask, "Will you be all right for a minute?"

"Yes, Joe's here," Jenny said, clinging to Joe's hand as he hovered protectively beside her.

Alan and Dorothy moved a short distance away.

"Do you think he's going to make it?" Dorothy asked, worried about the man who'd sacrificed himself to protect Jenny.

"I hope so, but the EMTs weren't talking."

She nodded slowly, painfully, remembering the horror that had just taken place.

"Dorothy—" Alan began seriously.

She looked up at him.

"I'm sorry for what I've done," he said, truly repentant. "What just happened"—he paused, his emotions unsettled—"what just happened," he began again, "made me realize how much you mean to me. If you'd been hurt today, if anything had happened to you, I would never have forgiven myself. We had something real good, and I ruined it. Is there anything I can do? Anything that will make things better for us?"

Dorothy was shocked by his confession and his apology. "We did have something good—and we had it for so long," she mourned.

"I want to do whatever it takes to make things right for us again. Will you give me a chance?"

"I don't know. We'll see," was all she could answer.

Alan nodded. He understood her reaction, but he was also firm in his conviction that he would win back her love. It wouldn't be easy. He didn't deserve her love, but he wouldn't quit trying.

Knowing he had nothing to lose, Alan reached out to take her hand.

Dorothy did not resist.

Joe stayed with Jenny on the steps as she spoke with the police officer. When the policeman moved away to talk with some of the other witnesses, Joe noticed she suddenly went very pale and seemed to sway unsteadily on her feet.

"Are you feeling all right?" he asked, concerned.

"No," she gasped.

He put an arm around her to steady her. "What is it? What's wrong?"

"I think I may need to go to the hospital."

"You were hurt? Why didn't you say something sooner! The EMTs could have looked at you—"

"It's the baby—"

"Officer!" Joe took charge.

The policeman looked his way.

"We have another emergency! She needs to get to the hospital!"

"Is there time to call an ambulance?"

Joe didn't hesitate. "No!"

The officer hurried over to help Joe escort Jenny down the steps to his patrol car.

Dorothy saw what was happening and hurried down to speak with them. "Can I do anything? How can I help you?"

Jenny looked up gratefully. "Could you call Mark for me?"

"Yes."

Jenny gave Dorothy Mark's number as she settled painfully into the back seat of the police car.

"I'll follow you in my car," Joe assured Jenny.

She gave him a heartfelt appreciative look. "Thanks."

Father Walters had seen Jenny being helped into the car and he went to check on her. "What's wrong?"

"We don't know, but the officer is going to take her to the hospital," Dorothy said.

"Is anyone going to be with her?"

"I am," Joe told him.

"Jenny, we'll be praying for you," he said, more worried now that he'd seen how pale she was.

"Thank you, Father."

The policeman got in the car and turned on his lights. They pulled away from the curb, siren wailing.

Joe and Father Walters shared a troubled look.

"Call me the minute you hear anything."

"I will," Joe promised.

Now that he knew Jenny was on her way to the hospital, Father Walters hurried back inside.

He had to find Darrell's phone number.
He had to call Claire.

Jenny sat in the backseat of the police car, trembling and terrified. Her pain was nearly constant, and she was suddenly terribly afraid for her baby.

CHAPTER
TWENTY-EIGHT

Go in peace to love and serve the Lord—

"It is with great joy we celebrate today," Father Walters said as he stood before those gathered at Our Lady. "We have been through a great trial together, but by our love for one another we have been made stronger."

Mark looked over at Jenny, who was sitting beside him, and knew the priest's words were true. When he'd gotten the call on that fateful day about Jenny's close call with death, Mark had been horrified. He had rushed to the hospital to be with her. Since that moment, he had come to realize just how precious the gift of life truly was. He had come so close to losing her that he wanted to live his life to the fullest now.

And Jenny was his life—Jenny and their son.

Mark's gaze dropped to the sleeping infant she held cradled in her arms, and his heart swelled with love. He had never known joy so sweet as the first moment he'd held their child. His delivery had been harrowing, but he was healthy and, of course, perfect.

Jenny sensed Mark's gaze upon her, and she looked his way. Her love for him was shining in her eyes. It was true they had been through some hard times, but as Father Walters had said, it had made their love stronger.

Margo sat on the other side of Mark, watching them, her heart filled with love. She was again humbled by all that had happened, and truly thankful that Mark and Jenny were together. She was especially thankful for her grandson. His birth had given her a whole new perspective on what was really important in life. She would not forget again.

In the pew behind them, Joe sat with Gail, holding hands. Though they had been married for all these years, their love had not lessened. If anything, it had grown in understanding and compassion. They knew they were blessed to have one another, and they never ceased to be thankful for that blessing.

Donna was there, too, looking on. She was thrilled Jenny had asked her to be godmother.

Alan and Dorothy were also there, wanting to celebrate this special moment with the proud parents. Dorothy had worried about Jenny when she'd been rushed off to the hospital. She'd been thrilled when she'd learned that everything had turned out all right.

There were several families present for the baptism today. The church was fairly crowded.

Father Walters began the rite with an introductory greeting and a prayer. After the Gospel reading and homily, the parents and godparents were asked to stand and reject sin and profess their faith in the Holy Trinity.

"Parents and godparents—if you will come to the baptismal font now," Father Walters directed.

Everyone filed out into the main aisle.

Jenny cradled her baby to her as she and Mark stood with Donna and Joe by the font.

When all had gathered around, Father blessed the water. He then asked both parents and godparents to put their hands upon the baby as the actual baptism was taking place. He came to Jenny and Mark first.

"Darrell Grant Seton," Father Walters said, "I baptize you in the name of the Father and the Son and the Holy Spirit." He poured the holy water over the sleeping infant's head.

Darrell didn't stay asleep for long.

The cold water being poured on his head evoked a cry from him.

Everyone in the church smiled.

Father anointed Darrell with chrism, then presented Jenny and Mark with a white bib as a sign of the baby's purity.

"Receive the light of Christ," Father said, handing them a candle that had been lighted from the Easter candle. He moved on to baptize the next infant.

Seated in a nearby pew with Claire by his side, Darrell looked on as his namesake was baptized. He was still recovering from his wounds and wasn't strong enough yet to stand for any length of time, but he hadn't been about to miss Darrell's baptism today.

He had been deeply touched and greatly honored when Jenny and Mark had come to him in the hospital and told him of their plan to name their son after him. Since then, he'd learned Jenny and Mark would also be attending the same marriage preparation classes at church that he and Claire were enrolled in.

Darrell would never have believed all those weeks ago that his life could have changed so completely—and for the better. Sergeant Williams and Stan Schmidt had visited him in the hospital and had given him the news that the killers had been caught, and that during interrogation, the gunmen had revealed the identity of the bad cop. The cop had been arrested and would pay for his crimes. Darrell had never said a word to anyone else, but he had learned that day that Sergeant Williams's first name was Michael.

Darrell turned his gaze to the altar.

He silently thanked God for all his blessings.

Father Walters is right—our love for one another does make us stronger.

Dear Readers,

Haven is the book of my heart. It's a story of real people trying to live their faith in the real world. When I started writing *Haven* ten years ago, I wanted to create a story that showed how love and a true faith in God could help my characters triumph over adversity. I've used the pseudonym Julie Marshall for *Haven*, because the storyline is different from my historical novels.

While the road to publication for *Haven* has been a long one—I've written eighteen other novels during that time—I always had faith that one day I would see it in print.

And now that day has finally come.

I'd like to thank my editor, the brilliant Alicia Condon, for believing in *Haven*, and Leisure Books for publishing it.

I hope you enjoy *Haven*.

Best always,
Bobbi Smith

BRAZEN
BOBBI SMITH

Casey Turner can rope and ride like any man, but when she strides down the streets of Hard Luck, Texas, nobody takes her for anything but a beautiful woman. Working alongside her Pa to keep the bank from foreclosing on the Bar T, she has no time for romance. But all that is about to change....

Michael Donovan has had a burr under his saddle about Casey for years. The last thing he wants is to be forced into marrying the little hoyden, but it looks like he has no choice if he wants to safeguard the future of the Donovan ranch. He'll do his darndest, but he can never let on that underneath her pretty new dresses Casey is as wild as ever, and in his arms she is positively...*BRAZEN.*

WANTON SPLENDOR
BOBBI SMITH

From Christopher Fletcher's simmering gaze to his lean strength, he infuses heat throughout Kathleen Kingsford's body. Caught amid her brother's foolishness and her enemy's greed, Katie longs for the solace Christopher promises. But can she trust this high-stakes gambler? As a vicious hurricane descends, she has no choice.

Katie appears at his door, her dress clinging to every curve, raindrops tracing tantalizing paths across her creamy skin. Ever since their first meeting, he wanted to be the one to protect her. And now she is here. Now she is his. Now they can finally surrender to their wanton splendor.

Dorchester Publishing Co., Inc.
P.O. Box 6640
Wayne, PA 19087-8640

52498-8
$5.99 US/$7.99 CAN

LONE WARRIOR
BOBBI SMITH

Marisa Williams learns how untamed the frontier can be when a party of raiding Comanche spirits her away to their village. Once there, they strip her and send her to a tipi to await her fate. When a virile warrior enters, she fears the worst. But his green eyes calm her fears, until his searing kiss enflames a passion that sets her shaking all over again.

Wind Ryder knows what being a captive of the Comanche means. Since he was taken many springs ago, he's become the best of warriors. The chief's gift of the blond beauty proves his prowess, but her silky skin and tender lips also haunt his dreams. Dreams that make Wind Ryder realize Marissa is the fiercest fighter of all, for she has won the battle for his his heart.

Bobbi Smith · SECRET FIRES · The Half-Breed

In the midst of the vast, windswept Texas plains stands a ranch wrested from the wilderness with blood, sweat and tears. It is the shining legacy of Thomas McBride to his five living heirs. But along with the fertile acres and herds of cattle, each will inherit a history of scandal, lies and hidden lust that threatens to burn out of control.

Chase knows he has no legitimate claim to the Circle M. After all, his father made it painfully clear he wants nothing to do with his bastard son or the Comanche girl he once took to his bed. But Chase has his own reasons for answering Tom McBride's deathbed summons. He has a job to do as a Texas Ranger, and a woman to protect—a woman whose sweet innocence gives him new faith that love born in the darkest night can face the dawn of all his tomorrows.

___4853-1 $5.99 US/$6.99 CAN

Dorchester Publishing Co., Inc.
P.O. Box 6640
Wayne, PA 19087-8640

Please add $2.50 for shipping and handling for the first book and $.75 for each book thereafter. NY, NYC, and PA residents, please add appropriate sales tax. No cash, stamps, or C.O.D.s. All orders shipped within 6 weeks via postal service book rate. Canadian orders require $2.50 extra postage and must be paid in U.S. dollars through a U.S. banking facility.

Name_____
Address_____
City_____ State_____ Zip_____
I have enclosed $ _____ in payment for the checked book(s).
Payment <u>must</u> accompany all orders. ❑ Please send a free catalog.
CHECK OUT OUR WEBSITE! www.dorchesterpub.com

BRIDES OF DURANGO: TESSA

BOBBI SMITH

Tessa Sinclair owns the local boarding house where she not only takes care of her guests, but every unfortunate she comes across. Brimming with compassion, Tessa is so busy rescuing other people she doesn't notice the dangers she continually faces—but marshal Jared Trent does. In fact, he notes every move the willful beauty makes. The most daring of all being the position she takes up in his heart. Tessa prides herself on seeing the best in everyone, but Jared Trent's determination to curtail her activities sorely tests her patience. As handsome as he is infuriating, Jared unearths feelings Tessa has never experienced before. And as he helps extract her from one perilous situation after another, she realizes she wouldn't mind getting caught in some close encounters with the dashing lawman himself—little dreaming he will unveil the love of a lifetime.

___4678-4 $5.99 US/$6.99 CAN

BRIDES OF DURANGO: ELISE

BOBBI SMITH

Elise Martin will do anything for a story—even stage a fake marriage to catch a thief. Dressed in a white lace gown, she looks every bit the bride, but when her "fiancé" fails to show, she offers ten dollars to the handsome gentleman who just stepped off the stage to pose as the groom. As a fake fiancé, he is all right, but when he turns out to be Gabriel West, the new owner of her paper, the *Durango Star*, Elise wants to turn tail and run. But she can't forget the passion his unexpected kiss at their "wedding" aroused, and she starts to wonder if there is more to Gabriel West than meets the eye. For the more time they spend together, the more Elise wonders if the next time she says, "I do" she just might mean it.

___4575-3 $5.99 US/$6.99 CAN